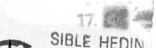

LIGHT OF EVENING

A thought-provoking novel, written with deep awareness of
the plight of a woman who suddenly finds herself in a totally
alien world. Sophie Brent, in early middle age and disappointed in marriage, leaves her home, husband and son
for life with an unreliable yet challenging and attractive older
man. Her experiences which follow—taking her to London,
Chicago and the South of France—make it often seem as if
she has jumped out of the frying pan into the fire. Yet,
trapped by Alexander Dolan's irresistible fascination, she
goes on. Sophie learns to live, but at a price. That price is
movingly portrayed, revealing the author's skill in handling a
complex set of characters in an even more complex situation.
One suffers with Sophie: love, failure, hope, loneliness,
desire, jealousy, ambition, guilt, depression and depen-
dency. Which emotion takes precedence is the theme of this
book.

By the same author

My Father, A. G. Street
Portrait of Wiltshire
Arthur Bryant: Portrait of a Historian

Light of Evening

A NOVEL

by

PAMELA STREET

ROBERT HALE · LONDON

© *Pamela Street 1981*
First published in Great Britain 1981

ISBN 0 7091 9251 7

Robert Hale Limited
Clerkenwell House
Clerkenwell Green
London EC1R 0HT

Photoset by
Kelly Typesetting Limited
Bradford-on-Avon, Wiltshire
Printed in Great Britain by
Clarke, Doble & Brendon Ltd.
Plymouth, Devon and
bound by Butler & Tanner Ltd.

"Two fears alternate in marriage, of
loneliness and of bondage. The dread
of loneliness being keener than the
fear of bondage, we get married."

"Complete physical union between two
people is the rarest sensation which
life can provide . . . Who escapes this
heaven may never have lived, who exists
for it alone is soon extinguished."

1

"If you go now," he said, "don't expect me to be around if you want to come back."

She looked down over the bay and then at the telegram in her hand, a message, as it seemed, from another existence: a piece of paper with the power to jerk her back three years, no, three years and three months, to be precise.

"But he's ill, Vincent. I always promised . . ."

"He made *you* ill enough, didn't he?" She noticed his eyes narrow, his face harden. The fierce Mediterranean sun shone relentlessly on the scene spread-eagled before her: dark green cypress and deep blue sea, white-bright villa and dusty road, the strange pink agglomeration of apartments near the coast stretching inwards across the valley like some octopus, a property-developer's dream devouring the natural beauty of the place. If only she could paint it as she had hoped, it would be her most ambitious picture yet. She couldn't quite explain it but she wanted to call it *Exploitation*. Exploitation was something she knew something about.

Somewhere far below them a dog barked. Then there was silence: hot, oppressive, ugly almost.

Presently he said, "I'll leave you to make up your mind, Sophie."

She watched him walk away down the narrow, winding path, his tall and surprisingly youthful figure in jeans and white shirt disappearing from time to time behind the trees. And she thought in a detached kind of way: 'I suppose I'm a bitch. He's so nice, so good-looking. I'm so lucky to have him, I owe him so much and yet . . .' She looked again at the telegram he had brought her, "So ill Dishy. So needing you. Alex". What was it she had said at their final meeting when she had seen the look in his eyes after she had made it plain she was leaving? "Of course, if you ever really needed me, Alex . . . If you were ill or anything, I'd come." What had made her? Pity? Love? Neither, exactly. She had felt during those last few weeks that she hated him. Even so, perhaps she had still wanted a loophole, a respectable one, that is.

Mechanically, she collected up her camp-stool and drawing materials, the rough beginnings of *Exploitation* barely decipherable on the sketch-pad. She might never get the picture on to canvas, not now, not if she went. The show in Paris which she had set her heart on might never take place. It would be like all the other things Alex had managed to wreck, quite unintentionally. But he had wrecked them all the same, like a small boy accidentally knocking down someone else's carefully-built pile of bricks on the nursery floor, as he rushed across it intent on his own pursuits. He didn't mean to do it. He was just wilful, greedy. Poor dear, lovable, hateful Alex who, when he was good was so very, very good, but when he was bad: absolutely bloody.

And it wouldn't only be *Exploitation* and her show he would be wrecking now. Guiltily, she realised that she had put her painting before the thing which should have been infinitely more precious: Vincent. He had said he wouldn't be around if she went and she knew him well enough to know that he meant it, unreasonable as it seemed. For after all, Alex must be over seventy now and possibly dying. She

might be gone only a very short time. It was unjust, cruel
even. But then Vincent, who was one of the kindest and
most reasonable people she had ever known, became
almost a different human being where Alex was concerned.

The villa greeted her, cool and dark after the brightness
outside, disturbing in its emptiness. There was no sign of
Vincent anywhere. It was like him to keep his word about
letting her make up her mind alone. For a moment she
toyed with the idea of putting a call through to England—
then rejected it. God knew what sort of a ménage Alex kept
now and there seemed something faintly ungracious about
such an act, as if she were doubting him all over again. A
telegram such as he had sent after all this time demanded
the kind of answer he would expect: extravagant, extreme,
unequivocal. She was touched that he should have remembered her words, turned to her, and so meticulously given
every detail of her present address. Sophie looked at her
watch. There was a man at the local travel agency who was
quite good at getting one fixed up quickly.

Everything became automatic now. She wasn't conscious
of having come to any decision. She was simply arranging
with the utmost calm to be at Nice airport by five o'clock or
1700. She always had a job synchronizing the times in her
own mind. Alex had been bad at it, too. Brilliant as he was,
it was one of his many blind spots. He used to argue that the
whole set-up was "monstrous" or "ridiculous". Of course,
he laid it on, but with his tremendous powers of persuasion
and oratory he could almost make anyone think that 1400
was really twelve or three. Could he possibly be dying?
Why should she bother? Why should she go? He'd ruined
her life enough, hadn't he, as Vincent had said. Was she
really going to let him ruin it for ever? What did a few
minutes by his bedside mean in the face of, say, another
twenty years, alone? After all, she was getting on now—
well on the downward slope. Was she really intending to
commit a sort of suicide for the sake of a promise to a man
who rarely kept any of his? A promise to a man who had
only to whisper "Dishy" on the telephone and she would
come running . . . running into his arms, sometimes
having to check herself when they were in public, especially

at the beginning. Not that Alex himself cared for the proprieties, often seeming—or pretending to seem—unaware that there were any.

The taxi came for her at four and by then she was packed and ready. She left a note for Ginette asking her to care for Monsieur as she had unexpectedly had to go to England. She did not leave a note for Vincent because she did not know what to say. In any case, he hated histrionics. She was quite unaware that, when the taxi bearing her to the airport drew away from the front door, he was sitting on the bank at the top of the garden, watching. She was conscious only of one thing: Alex. Alex needed her. Almost, it was as if the heat was on again.

As the plane rose, banked, and turned towards England, something inside her seemed to rise with it, something she had not felt for a very long time. She might have been back where it all began. Oddly enough, when she came to think about it, Alex must have been ill then, or mildly so. Otherwise he would never have been in that Harley Street doctor's waiting-room and Jamie, her son, would not have been able to point a finger at him and say, in a high-pitched embarrassing way, "Why's that man got a little pixie with him, Mummy?" To which Alex had replied, with complete composure, "He is my mascot, child. His name is Hob. You may play with him if you like."

Sophie opened her handbag and felt inside. Hob was still there. Hard and round and made of wood, the one tangible link with a period of heaven and hell. Much more hell than heaven towards the end. That was when she had once said, sensing—though trying not to—the inevitable, "Supposing we ever broke up, Alex, might I keep Hob?"

Her fingers closed over the smooth, squat, reassuring little form. Presently she drew him out and looked at him, his head a little to one side, a quizzical expression on his face, a face which was not altogether unlike Alex's. Poor Hob. Had he missed his former owner even more than she? Had he found it a greater upheaval when they had both started out together on a completely new way of life? She knew that Alex had always invested him with human qualities. Perhaps she should never have hung on to him. Posted him back in the box in which Alex had presented him to her. It was odd to think that it was Hob who had started the whole thing off. So long ago. She shut her eyes and the scene lay before her, startling in its clarity. That was the trouble about having a picture-book memory. Some of the etchings would never fade.

2

"Hob is a very special sort of person," Alex had explained, when Jamie sidled round the table to where he was sitting with a conglomeration of writing materials spread out on the long, conventional waiting-room table.

"Why?" Like most children, Jamie was uncomfortably direct.

Alexander Dolan regarded him over the top of his half-moon spectacles.

"There are two reasons," he replied, slowly. "He helps to look after me and he was given me by a lady."

The other inhabitants of the waiting-room suddenly began to take an interest. An elderly woman in the corner laid down her magazine. A middle-aged man smiled. Sophie said, "Jamie, come here. You mustn't be a nuisance."

"It's quite all right. Hob likes attention." Alex looked across at Sophie and she thought: what an ugly man. He must be fairly old—well into middle age, anyway. Rather high-handed of him to be monopolising the table like this.

I'm sure I've seen his photograph somewhere or other.

When the secretary came in and said, "Mr Alexander Dolan", she realised that he must be the artist, the man whose portraits she always admired so much. Soon afterwards she and Jamie were also summoned and she forgot all about him while she went into, for what seemed like the hundredth time, the bronchial-asthmatic condition with which her son had been afflicted, almost since birth. Until now, it had always been the same. She would start off with each new specialist with highest hopes. New remedies would be prescribed; new régimes tried. Occasionally, for a time, they would appear to work. Jamie would look quite well, his attendance at school miraculously regular; and then, suddenly, with hardly any warning, nemesis appeared in the form a curious pallor round Jamie's lips, a tell-tale wheeze, dark patches under the eyes, and they would be in for another session of desperate days, even more desperate nights, vomiting, antibiotics, special lamps and the seemingly eternal fighting for breath in a small, skinny frame whose every gasp appeared to be his last.

The latest doctor examined the child thoroughly, silently, then rang for his nurse and sent him out with her into another room. Turning to Sophie, he said, abruptly, "You must send him away."

"Away? But where?"

"Boarding-school."

"But he's not yet nine."

"A lot of children go much earlier."

"But Jamie's different. He's delicate."

"All the more reason."

There was a pause. He spoke more kindly. "Look, Mrs Brent. You're a conscientious mother, I'm sure. Probably too conscientious. You mean well. But actually you're Jamie's worst enemy. He would toughen up away from you. I assure you—these attacks would become less. You take my word for it."

She hadn't liked it. She collected Jamie and, in an ill-humour, went back to the waiting-room to pick up their respective belongings. She was surprised to find the Dolan man sitting once more at the table. He looked up as they came in, and smiled. "I thought your son might like to say good-bye to Hob."

"How kind." She was mollified. Had he waited for them? There was something appealing about him, for all his thick-set features and heavy, hunched body. His face, now animated, seemed transformed. There was almost a hypnotic quality about his eyes under their enormous bushy eyebrows. The three of them left the waiting-room together and as they reached the front door he asked, casually, "Might I give you a lift anywhere? I've a car outside."

She hesitated. "Oh, no thank you. We're only going to Paddington. We'll find a taxi."

"You may not. It's the rush hour. Have you a long journey?"

"Bath," she replied, shortly. She often became off-hand when shy.

"I'm going to Cornwall, as it happens. Hop in. I'll drive you home."

He bundled them into an ancient Bentley and she prayed that Jamie would not be sick. Towards the end of the journey her mind kept operating on two levels: I'll have to ask him in for a drink. Or a meal? I'd like to. but there's only a small casserole and it's Heidi's day off. As it is, I'll have to get Jamie to bed and do some vegetables. Something tells me this man Dolan will be bored by domesticity.

For all his charm and easy conversation she was in awe of him, aware that a pretty but smallish house belonging to a country estate agent would hardly be in keeping with his way of life. When, a mile or two from home, she put the question, somewhat diffidently, "Would you like a drink?" she was beginning to hope he would refuse. The alacrity with which he accepted amazed her.

"I'd like one very much, thank you."

Once inside the house, she became flustered. Hugh was not yet home. She sent Jamie upstairs, showed Alex where the cloakroom and sitting-room were and went into the kitchen to fetch ice and glasses, glancing in the mirror on her way, dismayed at her somewhat disarrayed appearance.

Sophie Brent was then thirty-four, tall, willowy with a pale, heart-shaped face, large brown eyes and a mass of natural, wavy auburn hair which, because she had—with considerable diffidence—asked for the windows in the car to be open as much as possible for Jamie's sake, was now falling about her shoulders and making her look, had she realised it, ten years younger. She had always seemed curiously unconscious of herself as a woman. She dressed well, had a natural flair for making herself look as attractive as possible, yet there was something remote about her. Some people considered her a little fey. Men admired her, but from a distance. She was therefore not only astonished but also disconcerted when, as soon as she returned to the sitting-room, Alexander Dolan wheeled round from the painting he was studying and said, "Has anyone ever told you that you're quite beautiful?"

She hesitated. "No."

"But surely, your husband . . ?"

"No, not really."

"He must be a moron." He stood there looking at her and she began to feel uncomfortable. There was an intensity, an urgency about him which seemed to fill the room. His presence was disturbing. She turned away and put the tray she was carrying down on a small side table.

"Would you like to help yourself?"

"Thanks. Incidentally, who did the portrait of your son over the fireplace?"

"I did."

"Then what, in heaven's name, are you doing in a set-up like this?"

Life had never seemed quite the same after that. In the weeks and months to come he made several attempts to see her. He rang, wrote and once, when she was out, called unexpectedly at the house. When she returned, Hugh said at dinner, "Oh, by the way, a most odd man, middle-aged, a bit like a tramp, called here asking for you."

"Oh?"

"Said he was interested in your paintings or something like that. Didn't know how he could have seen any."

Casually, she replied, "I expect it was the artist man who

gave Jamie and me a lift back from Harley Street some time ago. I forgot to tell you. He came in for a drink and happened to admire the one of Jamie in the sitting-room."

"Oh, I see." There was no curiosity, not even a faint interest that someone should have taken a good view of his wife's painting. To Hugh, her aspirations in that direction had initially seemed a pleasant hobby for his fiancée to indulge in, but after marriage an increasingly unnecessary and irksome pastime which interfered with the purpose for which he had married her, which was to further his own career.

They finished their meal in silence and afterwards she pleaded a headache and went upstairs to bed. She did not see Alexander Dolan again for eight years.

3

Sophie first went to Alexander's home in London on one of
the hottest summer afternoons that she could ever
remember. She was not surprised to find herself going
there because, somewhere in the depths of consciousness,
she had always felt that she would. She knew it was quite
ridiculous to think this—after all, she had virtually run
away from him, hadn't she?—but there had seemed such
an inevitability about their meeting which made her almost
certain that one day she would see him again. Her beliefs,
invariably illogical and arrived at only by some vague
process of osmosis, had an uncanny way of often proving
correct.

For eight years she had allowed such an idea to lie more or
less dormant, hardly daring to acknowledge something for
which she both hoped and feared. She had known at once
that Alexander Dolan spelt danger. He had aroused in her
the same fierce response which she had experienced only
once or twice before, a response which she had managed—
not without almost superhuman effort and self-discipline—

to suppress. She could imagine the look of horror on her widowed mother's face had she, in her youth, brought home the dissolute, middle-aged tutor at the local art college, or gone away for a weekend with the old roué who hunted the local hounds. Such behaviour was not even to be thought of. It was not in the scheme of things which Mrs Olivia Frampton of Hedley Manor had for her only daughter. That the latter had opted for and, at the age of twenty-three, married—out of, as Sophie now saw it, desperation—Hugh Brent, thereby finally causing greater distress to both mother and daughter, was something which, again, she preferred to leave unacknowledged.

It was not always possible, of course. Since meeting Alex again she had found herself thinking more and more about Hugh and their marriage. Moments of brutal honesty kept forcing themselves like indecent exposures into her more conditioned thoughts. What would he do or say now if he knew she was about to spend the afternoon with that "artist man" in order to let him paint her? At least, that was what Alex had said. The temperature in the railway carriage, combined with her own nervousness, made her uncomfortable and restless. Twice, she got up and stood in the corridor. When, at Reading, an unctuous voice flooded the platform with "Paddington only, this train. Paddington only," she almost descended to take the next one home. The puritanical principles with which, all her life, she had been so heavily overburdened and which were so totally at odds with those underlying forces within, tormented her. Nurture fought nature. Yet even as one part of her mind was telling her to get out while the going was good, she knew that the other was the stronger, that it would propel her, irresistibly, inescapably, to Number 29, St Anne's Square. Odd that nature seemed to have much more power of late. Was it age? A feeling of missing something she had so long wanted? Finding out before it was too late? And after all, said the conscience-calming little demon inside, you haven't actually *done* anything wrong yet, have you? Is it really such a sin not to have mentioned to your husband that you had run into that artist man at the private view of a friend's paintings the previous week? That he had taken hold of both your hands and told you that you were more beautiful than ever? You don't have to account for all your actions, all that happens to you now, surely to God? You're middle-aged. Your son is almost grown-up. Why blame yourself for craving something Hugh can't give you? Wasn't he far more deceitful himself all those years ago? She remembered so well the last night of their honeymoon, how he had sat on the end of the bed while she had lain back on the pillows wearing what she had hoped might have proved an irresistibly seductive nightdress. "I'm afraid I've been a rather disappointing lover, Sophie." And she had stared at him and said, "What exactly do you mean, Hugh?" His eyes had slewed away, the expression on his face enigmatic, uneasy. "I'll tell you, sometime. Not now. It'll be better, I promise. You'll see."

He hadn't told her until much later. By then Jamie had been conceived and she had tried to forget what he had said by preparing, with increasing nervousness and dismay, for motherhood. How long ago all that seemed, that life, as it were, now twice removed, those terrifying bouts of child-hood illness, those sleepless nights, those seemingly inter-minable trips to doctors, hospitals, specialists up and down the length of Harley Street. Odd though, that one of them should have brought her Alex.

She had been so intent on seeing him again that she had hardly given a thought as to what his home might be like. Now, she found herself suddenly confronted by a room at the top of a house so high and white and bright that, when he led her out on to a little balcony, she had a dizzy feeling that she might be on board ship, full steam ahead. Beneath an all-blue sky, rooftop London seemed to be shimmering. After the heat of the streets a small breeze teased round the chimney pots. She shivered slightly.

"Come back inside and see Hob." He took her arm, gently. "Would you like some tea? Or shall we get down to work?" So he really did mean to paint her, after all? She told herself not to be disappointed. *Stop acting like like a fool, Sophie. You're a big girl now.*

She picked up his little mascot and fingered it thought-fully, remembering. "Perhaps it would be best to start. I haven't a lot of time."

"Really?" He looked at her in an amused way. "Well, we'll see how it goes, shall we? Perhaps you'd like the bathroom or something, but for God's sake don't tidy your hair. I like it the way it is. Your dress is nice."

"Thank you."

She sat for him for almost an hour before he said, quite suddenly, "That's enough for today. Why are you so tense?"

"I wasn't aware that I was."

"No?" Again, the amused expression. "I'll get some tea now."

"Can I help?"

"Tea-making is not beyond my powers. But you can fill the kettle if you like. Through there."

She went into a small adjoining room where there was a tap and a sink. Its disorderliness neither surprised nor dismayed her, although had it been her own home she would have wanted to set to work on it at once.

They drank their tea out of mugs, almost in silence, a silence which was all the more disconcerting in that he appeared to make no attempt at helping her to break it. The afternoon had somehow not been at all what she had expected and she had a feeling he was perfectly well aware of this, that he was almost enjoying her discomfiture.

"I'll have to go soon."

"Back to purdah?"

"Please. What makes you say that?"

"It's just that you strike me as being the most unsuitable woman for the role you so valiantly try to adopt. Now, let's see. Next week I shall be down in Cornwall. Would today fortnight, the 27th, suit you?"

"Yes. Yes, I think so." His matter-of-factness annoyed her. She felt tired and deflated. Apart from his somewhat pertinent remarks, he had behaved most decorously. She had evidently simply interested him as a woman he wanted to paint. She might have been paying him to do so. Perhaps he was even expecting that she would. Nothing had been said about money.

"Don't look so disappointed, my dear." He could have

been talking to a child. She knew he was teasing her and she flushed, angry that he could see through her so easily.

"That's better. You're much prettier when the aggression comes out." He leaned forward and took her empty mug away. Afterwards, she was never quite sure exactly how it came about that his arms were round her, his hands moving over her body to places where Hugh's had never begun to trespass, and his voice—seemingly from a long way off—was saying, "Isn't this what you've been waiting for, Sophie? Ever since that Harley Street waiting-room?" She only knew that the whiteness of the room blurred, that another, altogether different, more carefree Sophie laughed and whispered, "Yes, it seems just what the doctor ordered."

It was almost nine o'clock before she arrived home.

4

"But I don't understand. You say you felt faint at Paddington?" Hugh was at his most pompous, wandering about waving a cigarette holder in one hand, holding a glass of whisky in the other. "Why didn't you telephone?"

"I've told you, I was feeling too faint. I just sat down in the waiting-room."

"Most peculiar. We'd better get Tillotson to run the rule over you in the morning."

"I don't want Tillotson to run the rule over me." She wished he wouldn't talk in clichés.

"Look here, Sophie. You went to London to do some shopping on the spur of the moment. It was, admittedly, a damn fool thing to do on such a hot day. But all the same, one can't ignore your feeling faint for so long a time. It's so unlike you. It's a bit late now, but I'll ring him first thing."

"I don't want you to ring him first thing. I shall be all right. Anyone can feel faint on occasions."

"You never have before, except . . ." He paused. "You're not pregnant, are you?"

"How could I be? Think of my age and anyway the last time we . . ."

"No. No, I suppose not. Incidentally, I was sorry you weren't here when I got back. because I had something rather special to tell you."

"Oh?" Was *that* why he was carrying on so? She hated herself for thinking it, but she had not been prepared for so much concern.

"You may not want to hear it now, but, well, I might as well tell you. I'm being made a senior partner and they want me to take on the London office."

"The *London* office?"

"You needn't make it sound as if it were in Mars."

"No. I'm sorry. I'm so pleased, Hugh. Honestly I am. Shall we live in London?"

"God no. But I think we must seriously think of getting a place a little nearer. Within reasonable commuting distance. We could, I suppose, have a small pied-à-terre in town later on."

"I see." They had already moved twice during the last few years, as Hugh's fortunes increased. Each time he had sold at a profit, just after all the improvements he had insisted on had been finished and she thought they were settled.

"You don't sound very enthusiastic."

"It's, well, just a bit of a shock, that's all."

"I told you I meant to get on, Sophie."

"Yes. I knew you would. I really am awfully glad, Hugh."

"Incidentally, I'd like to ask the Beresfords down for a weekend. He's the chap I'll be taking over from in London. I was talking to him on the 'phone today. I said I'd have to confirm with you, of course, but tentatively I suggested they came down a fortnight this Friday, the 27th."

"The *27th*?" Her voice was high-pitched, incredulous. The hand which held her drink suddenly jerked and a little of the liquid spilled over on to her skirt. Fortunately he had had his back to her, but he turned suddenly, a puzzled expression on his face.

"There's nothing wrong with the 27th, is there? I felt sure we had nothing on then."

"Yes we have. I mean, I have. I've got a dental appointment."

"For heaven's sake, Sophie. You can put that off, surely. It's probably only a routine thing, isn't it?"

"No." She was in control of herself again now, surprised at how easily lie followed lie. "I'm going to have a molar crowned. I want to get on with it. Before Jamie's speech day. Why can't the Beresfords come a little later on?"

"Because he's going to have an operation, that's why. There's a bit of an urgency about the whole thing."

"I should have thought it might have been better if you'd simply gone to see him in London."

He frowned, sat down suddenly and stared into his glass. "You're not yourself, Sophie. I'm sorry I mentioned all this tonight. We'll talk about it again in the morning. If you really don't want a meal, I think you should go to bed."

He was dismissing her, as a school-teacher might do a fractious child. She wasn't being amenable, not the charming, attractive wife, his number one asset whom he wanted the Beresfords to meet. She looked at him across the room, a space of a few feet which might have been the Sahara Desert. He had put on weight lately, his once-spare figure had thickened considerably around the waist. His face was more jowled, the dark wavy hair receding. Was it really possible that she was married to this man, that he was the father of her child, that he still, on occasions, performed the same act with her which Alex had done a few hours earlier, an act that, for want of a better expression, was known as "making love", but which, in the unbelievable dissimilarity in the way it was carried out should never, surely, have been given such an unsuitable connotation.

"Good night, Hugh." She put down her glass, left the room and went upstairs. They had ceased, long ago, to share a bedroom. She took a long, hot bath and then lay in bed staring at the ceiling. Presently, she heard him come to bed also and go into his dressing-room. She was aware of him brushing his teeth for what seemed an inordinate length of time, the lavatory flushing, a window opening, all the ritualistic noises that went on with cohabitation and which increasingly irritated her. And she knew it would be the same the next night and the next one and the next, unless, of course, Hugh decided to make one of his rare visits to her bedroom. She had come to dread the light tap, the door opening, his silk-pyjama-clad figure moving swiftly across the room and the agitation and gyrations that followed which gave her no pleasure and, she suspected, only gave Hugh a modicum of satisfaction or relief.

Poor Hugh. It wasn't, she kept telling herself, his fault if he didn't have a very high sex drive, if the act didn't come more naturally to him. Should she not have been more understanding when, after drinking a little more than usual one night, he had at last admitted that, because of an isolated incident in his schooldays, he had, for a time, occasionally had certain feelings for men as well as women. He had apparently fought the former tendency, had never indulged it. It was obviously something he looked back on with guilt and distaste. It was, he assured her, a thing of the past, a phase of growing-up which many boys went through. Since marrying her all such inclinations had vanished.

She remembered having been appalled. She had been young and hopelessly ignorant. Although she had often puzzled over his lack of desire, regretted that he did not want to go to bed with her more frequently and that when they did it was not at all what she had been hoping for, it had never occurred to her that something like this might be the answer. Often she had fretted, wondering whether the fault lay with herself. How was she to know that he had repressed sex to such a degree that, for him, it had become a kind of necessary keep-fit exercise, not nearly as important as the necessity for doing well at his job, getting on, making money? No wonder that sexual intercourse seemed to embarrass him so much, that he found it, in some way, shocking.

And now, the sad and silly thing about it all was that, had Hugh witnessed her infidelity that afternoon, he would probably have been not only shocked at that, but probably even more at the delight with which she had abandoned herself. "Shocking", like "making love", meant different things to different people.

5

The Beresfords hung over the ensuing weekend as if they were actually present, large, menacing and, Sophie was sure, utterly boring. She could see him, fat, bald and telling stories throughout every meal, stories at which she would fail to laugh in the right places. Mrs Beresford would be blue-rinsed, a faded compliment to him. She would tell of children who were married or not married, grandchildren who were boys or girls, holidays in Majorca or Madeira, hotels where the service was good or bad. They would have to ask some people in to meet them. Who? Sophie was fierce in her loathing, as a child whose treat is threatened. Many years ago she might have lain on the floor and kicked and screamed.

She was therefore somewhat mollified when, on Sunday morning, the telephone rang and a calm, pleasant voice came on the line. "Mrs Brent? Frank Beresford here. I thought perhaps I should ring now about that weekend your husband so generously proposed." So Hugh had definitely asked them, had he? "I'm so sorry but I have to go into hospital sooner than expected. Next week, in fact. I'm afraid we won't be able to manage it after all . . ."

Relief flooded through her. She wanted to kiss Frank Beresford or the telephone, tell him how happy she was about his operation, how absolutely splendid it was that it was so urgent. Bloody woman that I am, said one part of her mind as the other made the expected, conventional platitudes, "I'm *so* sorry . . . We had *so* been looking forward to it . . . Perhaps when you're better . . . Yes, you must come then . . . Yes, I'll tell Hugh. No, he's not here. He's," she hesitated, "at the club."

She presumed that he was there because he had gone out in the car soon after breakfast. It was now twelve o'clock and that was where he often ended up before lunch on Sundays. There was an old house run by a retired major and his wife that called itself Greenacre Country Club which he seemed to frequent more and more, although he preferred it if she accompanied him. For all his superficial charm, she knew he lacked confidence, that her presence to him was important, that he wished to produce an attractive, well-dressed wife almost as part of his credentials. When, as so often, she had pleaded Jamie's ill-health or they had had a difference of opinion about something or other, as now, he had gone alone, returning pinker than usual and late for lunch.

Now, with her next visit to Alex once more assured, she did her best to be as agreeable as possible when Hugh returned at a quarter to two.

"So they can't come after all?"

"No. He'd like you to ring him tomorrow."

"Seems as if I'll have to take over sooner than we thought. We'd better start thinking about that move straight away. What sort of area do you fancy? Buckinghamshire? Or we might try Kent. I don't suppose you're all that keen on the Surrey stockbroker belt, are you?"

She was silent, trying to weigh up the implications. There would be so much to do. What would it all mean vis-à-vis her and Alex? Would it eventually be easier? Her sudden propensity for low scheming both amazed and appalled her. When Hugh had said that she wasn't herself, perhaps he had been right. Or was this other self the one she really was, the one who had fallen so wildly, wickedly and hopelessly in love with a man she hardly knew?

For, apart from his reputation as a painter, she knew virtually nothing about Alexander Dolan, the man. During the next few days she began wondering more and more about his journey to Cornwall, the place where, strangely enough, he had been going the first time they met. Did he have another home there? He had given no clue, no address. He might have been at the other end of the world. Who was he with? She swung between panic and pessimism. Supposing he didn't come back? Supposing she never saw him again? Perhaps he had just been playing with her. Testing her out. Seeing whether she was any good at . . .

"Waring and Abbotts on the telephone, Mrs Brent." She had not heard Heidi come across the lawn to where she was sitting, making conjecture after conjecture. She started violently. The girl looked at her curiously and turned back towards the house, Sophie quickly overtaking her, while doing her best to appear casual. So Alex had meant what he said when, after she had requested that he never telephoned her, he had protested, "But I might have to. I shall pretend to be someone else." "Who?" "Your bank manager." "My bank manager never rings me." "Your couturier, then." "I don't have one." "Oh, for Christ's sake, Sophie, "your chiropodist." "Do you imagine I have corns?" He had burst out laughing. "All right, you win. I shall be a shop. Surely you must order things occasionally from a *shop*."

His voice, when she picked up the receiver and said "Hello" was quite unrecognizable. "Mrs Brent?"

"Yes?"

"Ah, Stevens here, from Waring and Abbotts. The new mattresses have come in sooner than the date I gave you. I wondered whether you would like to try one, whether tomorrow might be convenient?"

She stifled her laughter. She could hear Heidi in the kitchen, whisking something. Suddenly the noise ceased. The girl had come to them when Jamie had been small and, fortunately, decided to stay. Although her English was still poor, Sophie had an idea she took in a great deal more than she would ever let them know.

"Tomorrow afternoon, then, Mrs Brent? About two?"

"Yes, I think that will be all right."

"It would be advisable not to wait any longer. I find they're going rather quickly."

"I quite understand. I don't want to wait . . ." The words were said before she could stop them.

There was a low chuckle. His voice returned to normal. "Neither do I, Mrs Brent. Neither do I. That's why I came back early."

6

"It's only a slight stroke, you understand, Mrs Brent. But I think you should come, all the same. She's asked for you."

"Of course. Tell her I'll be there"—she looked at her watch—"around five, or soon afterwards."

Sophie put down the receiver, ashamed that her first reaction had been one of relief: not relief that Dr Fellowes had testified to the mildness of her mother's condition, but relief that the news had not come on a day when she might, conceivably, have been going to see Alex. They had been meeting for several months now. Their passion showed no signs of abating.

She managed to telephone Hugh at his London club just before he was leaving for the office. He had taken to staying in town during the week—something which happened to be highly convenient from her point of view—but which irked him considerably, as did the fact that they had, as yet, failed to find a more convenient home from which he could commute. More than once he had accused her of not trying or being hyper-critical of anything he took her to see.

This morning, however, he seemed kinder and more understanding. "I'm sorry, Sophie. You'll take the car, I presume?"

"Yes." She loathed driving long distances alone, but this time there was no option if she was to get to Hedley Manor as promised. She had often suggested to her mother that she ought to move into a smaller, more easily-accessible place than the old Elizabethan house in a particularly remote part of Cheshire. But Olivia had been adamant. Her answers were always the same: she and her companion, Mrs Boxley, could perfectly well manage. This was where she had lived for over half a century and, God willing, this was where she was going to die. Then, after reaffirming her intentions, she would trail off into innuendoes, small grievances, ridiculous suspicions—"I am *sure*, Sophie, that Mrs Boxley has been at the sherry decanter"—invariably ending up by expressing her regret that her daughter lived *quite* so far away, "although I *do* understand, dear, how difficult it is for you to come *quite* so far *quite* as often as I'd hoped . . . what with *dear* Hugh and Jamie to think of . . ." Sophie wished she wouldn't stress the 'dear' before Hugh. She knew her mother hated him.

Now, as she began her long journey northwards, she was distressed to think she hadn't been to Hedley for over three months. She wondered what would have happened if she had paid more attention to what Olivia had said all those years ago, before the latter had finally, and with so much reluctance, consented to her daughter's engagement being announced in *The Times*. "You're throwing yourself away, Sophie . . . When I think who you might have married . . . I've never been able to understand why you haven't been more, well, *outgoing* . . . got around a bit . . . If only you hadn't been born at such an unfortunate time . . . If only you hadn't been eighteen just when the war ended, you could have had a season . . . I could have made you the deb of the year if you'd condescended to play your cards right . . ." Sophie remembered standing in the library at Hedley looking out on the sodden, wintry, Cheshire land-scape and replying, "Please don't go on so. I've made up my mind, although I do wish we didn't have to have a white wedding."

Had she been faced with the same questions today, would she have answered less equivocally? Why exactly *had* she married Hugh? Of course, he had been a good-looking young man and not without a certain charm, a kind of boyish enthusiasm. She had admired his desire to get on in the world. It had never occurred to her that, by marrying her, he was taking more than a few steps in the right direction. He had, moreover, seemed quite enthusiastic about her painting in those days, something for which, as she took it so seriously, she was grateful. They had even joked together about her having her own little "studio" in the home they envisaged. She felt he would be kind, would constitute no threat to her individuality. She would not be forever thinking that she would have to "live up" to someone else's idea of what she should or should not be like, that she would not be continually subjected to criticism—even critical analysis—as had been the case for so long with Olivia. And it was time she married. Most of the friends she had made at school, and the other more superficial ones she had got to know since, had by now found themselves a husband. All were surprised that Sophie Frampton—by any standards, one of the prettiest and most eligible among them—had so far failed in the marriage stakes.

Yet there was another reason, an underlying one which, only recently since knowing Alex, had she dared to bring out of the box in which she had successfully hidden so many secrets for so many years. It was the reason which had not only interfered with getting married but which had kept her, with all its frustrations and irritations, living at Hedley with Olivia when she might have migrated, like many of her contemporaries, to London. Soon after she had left school she had fallen for someone far more unsuitable than Hugh, someone whom she had happened to meet at one of the local charity functions over which Olivia was constantly presiding. He had paused to admire a small painting of Sophie's which was being sold to raise funds. Then he had returned and bought it. He was bald, fiftyish, large, untidy and spoke with a very faint foreign accent. Later, she discovered that he was a refugee from Germany who had come to England just before the war. Later still, she found out that he was married and also, if rumour was to be believed, lecherous. There was talk of him having attempted to seduce any reasonably good-looking pupil who came under his tutelage at the now re-opened art college to which—to Olivia's concern and disgust—Sophie insisted on going.

She had known, of course, that the whole thing was ridiculous, hopeless and deplorable. She was at a loss to understand herself. She pretended to shocked dismay on overhearing defamatory remarks to the effect that yet another victim had fallen like a ninepin before his skilled advances. How much truth there was in such allegations she never really knew. In his presence she remained cold and aloof. He himself invariably behaved impeccably towards her, something which, because she was not prepared to be honest with herself, left her constantly annoyed and, at times, even puzzled. It was always, "Miss Frampton, I think if you could be a little bolder in outline . . . Miss Frampton, I think you could afford to leave out the detail here. You're better at more impressionistic work . . . Ah, now this is *good*, Miss Frampton . . ."

Would she have succumbed if he had given her half a chance? She was still a virgin, in many ways painfully naïve and unsophisticated, for all the superficial "finishing" which her mother, chafing at not being able to do more owing to the exigencies of a post-war England, had imposed on her. Olivia had certainly sidestepped sex education. And her daughter had never been a girl to discuss that sort of thing with others. What exactly happened? How did one set about it? Supposing one got pregnant? How did one get "fixed up"? What would Olivia say if . . . It didn't bear contemplating. Miserably, she went on painting, longing for something, although she was not quite sure what.

Only once did her tutor give her any intimation that he had noticed her in a way not entirely connected with art. It was the end of the day when she had been getting into the car which Olivia sometimes lent her, when she felt she could spare enough petrol from her ration so that her daughter could transport herself, without having to resort

to a bus, to and from that "dismal place", as her mother
would keep referring to the college. He had been collecting
his own car which was parked near by. As he drew level he
paused and said, "Ah, good night, Miss Frampton. Back to
the manor born, I see." The pun seemed deliberate, provocative and cruel. Did she imagine in the half light that she
had seen the flick of his tongue as he smiled and raised his
battered hat?

Soon after that she had met Hugh. He had been her
escape. Poor Hugh. She had not treated him very well then
and she wasn't treating him very well now. In her new-
found ecstasy, his eager, restless searching for another
home seemed not only pathetic but doomed. Whatever he
did, wherever they went, it could only be a charade. How
long could she keep up the pretence? How long should
one . . ?

She had been thinking so hard that she missed a turning
near Stoke-on-Trent. It was almost six before she turned
into the long driveway to Hedley and swung the car round
by the front door. It opened almost immediately, Mrs
Boxley, like a small, grey, agitated pouter-pigeon, running
out to meet her.

"My dear . . ."

She noticed the ageing blue eyes were red-rimmed and
puffy.

"I'm so very sorry . . . a second stroke . . . this afternoon . . . There was nothing anyone could do."

7

"We could knock down this wall. Make a wide archway. Then we'd have a most attractive room, don't you think?"

Hugh paced about, as if already in possession, plans pouring out of him as they passed through one doorway after another in the long, low, empty farmhouse. He had brought her, of all places, to the borders of Essex and Suffolk, late one Friday afternoon. They were to spend the night at a hotel in Colchester.

"You'd still be sixty miles from London, Hugh."

He appeared not to hear, his eyes resolutely focused on some obscure part of the ceiling. Sophie walked across to the window and stared out at the flat, singularly featureless landscape. The day had been bleak and chilly. Rain clouds were now sweeping in from the direction of the North Sea. There was neither habitation nor human being in sight. Hugh couldn't ask her to live *here*, could he?

It appeared he could.

"It's an absolute snip, Sophie. No one else has seen it, yet. Given a year or two we could transform this place.

Increase its value tenfold. Think what you'd do with the garden."

Sophie did not want to think what she would do with the garden. She had already made or improved three during their married life. And this particular one was a wilderness.

"Why's it been empty so long?"

"Oh, I don't know. Sometimes happens. Previous owner took a long time dying in some nursing-home, I believe." He had begun walking back into the hall and up the stairs. She listened to his footsteps marching about determinedly overhead.

"Aren't you coming up?" His voice echoed over the banisters, alien and disembodied.

She followed unwillingly and found him standing in a large, dark room studying the heavy panelling with obvious approval. At times like these he had an aggravating habit of sucking his teeth, making little hissing noises like a horse-coper. She knew instinctively what he was about to say. He had said the same thing in almost every house they had ever looked at.

"This would be the master bedroom."

"Yes, I suppose so." Why was it always master? Why not mistress? She imagined lying there in a four-poster, and shivered.

"Hugh, I don't like this place. Bad atmosphere. It reminds me of Hedley. Let's go."

"But Darling . . ." He so rarely called her that nowadays. Did he think a sudden endearment was going to make her see things differently? God, how far apart they'd grown.

"I'm sorry, Hugh. I find it dreadfully depressing. I should hate to live here. In fact, I don't think I like Essex at all, not from what we've seen today."

"You're seeing it under bad conditions. The weather's foul. Wait till tomorrow. The sun might shine and you'll think differently."

She knew she would never think differently. Even though she might be that much nearer Alex, it was somehow the wrong side of London. All his journeys seemed to be westward. Nothing was going to make her settle down in such a god-forsaken spot as this. She turned to go, knowing that she had behaved badly.

At dinner back at the hotel she tried to make amends. They did not often spend a night away together and both seemed conscious that a special effort needed to be made. She was also acutely alive to the fact that Hugh had simply booked one double room and bath. Perhaps if she drank a little more . . ? He seemed surprised and then rather pleased when she asked for a whisky after dinner.

"You do realize," he said, coming back across the lounge with their drinks, "that there's a distinct possibility of acquiring some land with that house a little later on?"

"Yes, you did mention it. But what would you want it for?"

He paused. "Good investment. And I've sometimes felt that Jamie might like to farm."

"Oh, I *see*." She was beginning to see only too well. They had not discussed it very much but she was suddenly uncomfortably aware of what he was thinking. When Olivia's estate was wound up she knew she would be a comparatively rich woman. But she hadn't reckoned on Hugh expecting her to put whatever inheritance she had towards buying a *farm*.

"You haven't, naturally enough perhaps, given as much thought to Jamie's future as I have, Sophie."

"No, I suppose not. When he was small I was so keen on, well, just keeping him alive. And then I was so relieved when he began to toughen up at boarding school, just like that specialist said—you know, the one I didn't believe. I've never really thought all that much about what he's going to *do*. After he's been to college it's up to him, isn't it?"

Guiltily, she realised that she had hardly thought about Jamie at all lately. Or had she, perhaps, pushed him away in that private box of hers along with all the other conscience-smiting thoughts? For there was no doubt that an almost grown-up son was not quite in keeping with her present way of life. She remembered how bored and detached she had felt at his last Speech Day. Whatever would he have thought of his mother if he had known that the previous afternoon she had . . . The recollection brought heightened colour to her cheeks, a strange sensation throughout her body.

"But, of course, if you really don't think you could stand the place we saw today, there's always others. More fish in the sea, as they say." Hugh laughed, a little too forcedly. She knew he was trying, too. Trying to be conciliatory, hoping perhaps, against hope, that she would change her mind.

She went up to bed first and he followed half an hour later. It was, she reflected, a little like the first night of their honeymoon. She suspected that he had given himself time for another drink or two.

It seemed childish to feign sleep, so she merely lay in bed, antennae-stretched, listening while he went through his usual routine. Her fingers clenched and unclenched: now he's taking off his tie, now he's got to his shirt, his pants, he's going to fold them up—his neatness always unnerved her—now he's sliding his legs into his pyjamas, off to the bathroom, teeth, lavatory . . . Now he's coming back. There was a swish of curtains as he checked the windows. What next? She expected his bed to squeak and rustle a little. But it didn't. Suddenly, her whole body stiffened with awareness, aware that he was standing, no *kneeling*, beside her, one hand gently groping.

"Sophie . . ."

She sat up with such violence that the bedclothes were thrown in his face. He was transformed into a muffled, flailing, white-hooded monster. A Druid perhaps? Or a member of the Klu Klux Klan? She did not know whether to laugh or cry, to extricate him or flee to the bathroom. Then his face emerged, the expression on it one of reproachful bewilderment.

"I'm sorry, Sophie."

He got into his own bed. Hours, many hours later, she was relieved to hear him at last beginning to snore. Only then did she begin, quietly, to sob.

8

"So you didn't care for Essex, my love?"

"No."

"I didn't think you would. Too flat. You're an up-and-down girl." Alex ran his hand playfully over the ups and downs of her body. "Your husband would have had to erect a Hanging Garden of Babylon to keep you happy there."

"Nothing would have kept me happy there."

"No. Perhaps not."

He was silent. She was quite unprepared for his next remark.

"Do you think you'd be happier in the United States?"

"The *United States*?" She turned towards him quickly, propping herself on one elbow. He pulled her back beside him.

"Please lie quietly, Sophie. Sometimes you remind me of a frightened filly who has just spied a dangerous object and is about to shy—or bolt."

"But I don't understand."

"No. How could you. Most inconsiderate of me. Now

stay still and I'll tell you." He raised both arms and crossed
them behind his head.

"I'm going to Chicago, after Christmas, at the invitation—or request if you like—of a certain Mr Bradley J.
Stevens. I'll be away about three or four months, I should
think."

"Three or four *months?*" A sharp icicle of fear seemed to
hit her somewhere between the eyes and then trickle slowly
downwards throughout her whole being.

Ignoring her parrot-like repetition of his last words, he
continued, "Bradley J. is a very rich old gentleman, Sophie.
He usually comes to England each year, but now his doctors
have advised against it. I painted him when he was over
here some time ago and he was pleased with the result. It
now appears that his dearest wish is for me not only to paint
him again but also the second Mrs Bradley J.—she's called
Lucky, by the way—and the whole of the rest of his family.
And that's saying something. He had three children by his
first wife and after they all married it seems none of them
has been exactly infertile. There would appear to be a
dynasty out there. Founded on canned meat."

This time he paused, but she did not speak because she
wasn't quite sure how her voice would come out.

Presently he said, "Of course, it *mightn't* be as long as
three or four months. I tried to get him to postpone it all
until later on, but I think he's scared his days may be
numbered. It'll be bloody cold out there at that time of year,
although I daresay Bradley J. knows how to turn up the
heat. And it could interfere with some summer exhibitions
over here—particularly the Academy—although I suppose
I can get all that sorted out before I go. A lot will depend on
how everything works out, how many grandchildren are
rounded up from Washington, Tennessee or wherever.
Bradley J. has apparently got a guest-house on his vast
estate which I'm to have free use of for as long as I want.
Meals are all laid on. Drink. The lot . . ."

He paused. He had evidently given the matter a good
deal of thought. She realised negotiations must have been
going on for some time. She wondered why he had chosen
to tell her just now.

"The trouble with me, Sophie, is," he went on, "that I'm not awfully keen on America or Americans. The men all talk big business and the women gobble one up. I could be very lonely. I shall have to have an English rose, a *sexy* English rose, that is, to protect me."

Had she been less in love with him, more of a woman of the world, his last words might have acted as warning enough. He paused again and still she did not speak. He reached down and took one of her hands.

"Sophie, will you come with me?"

There was a tight feeling in her chest. She seemed to have difficulty in breathing. The nature-nurture war inside waged for approximately thirty seconds. Her voice came back to her but from a long way off.

"Yes, Alex."

"Good girl." He brought his other arm down, turned and began to make love to her again. It would be time to think, afterwards.

She did not really begin to do so seriously until she was on her way home. A few hours ago she seemed to have shed, like some chrysalis, a final skin. She had stepped, metaphorically, out of a marriage. The actual, physical, painful technicalities of such an act were things to be got over as best as she could. She would have to tell Hugh. And Jamie. When, exactly? She couldn't do it just before Christmas, but as soon as it was over . . . It was fortunate that Jamie was going ski-ing. She would talk to Hugh first. Her son needn't know until the end of the holidays. The problems were legion, yet she knew that if Alex had asked her the same question over again, her decision would not have been different.

They had talked about it but little before she left. Both, perhaps, had felt "sufficient for the day". In any case, she had known instinctively that Alex would leave it to her to work out her own particular problems alone. He had never enquired too deeply into her past or even present relationships. She had sensed from the beginning that he did not wish to be questioned about his. He was such a private person. He had told her so little about himself. He had mentioned, briefly, that he had been married, that it hadn't been a success and he and his wife were separated. From the way he spoke she guessed he had no time for that institution, although just before she had left that day he had remarked that it would probably be wisest, as long as she didn't mind, to call herself Mrs Dolan while staying with the Bradley Js. "Americans are funny. They have this ridiculous reverence for the married state, whatever goes on on the sidelines." Sometimes, she wondered fancifully, whether his semi-detached wife lived in Cornwall. He had been singularly unforthcoming about his visits there. "I've got this ramshackle old place—Tremarthen—on the cliffs . . . someone keeps an eye on it for me . . ." He had certainly gone less frequently of late, but then it was winter, although he appeared to be going down for Christmas.

Once or twice she had felt that he was about to tell her more and she had tried to keep the conversation going, but as soon as she had said something which she hoped might draw him out further, he had changed the subject, adroitly; and so she had given up trying. She was too scared of losing him to risk his displeasure. She knew that what mattered most to him was the here and now. Her visits brought him, so he said, more happiness, more delight, than he had known in his whole life. And although she felt this to be a miracle, his reaction each time she arrived gave her no reason to disbelieve him: "Oh Sophie, Darling, Oh, Frabjous day! I swear you're prettier every time you come through my front door. That dress is a dream. I've never known another woman who knew how to dress like you. But we'll take it off, shall we? I mean, that's what you want, isn't it? I do." And then nothing else seemed to matter. Nothing at all. The time she spent with him was something out of context, apart. She was never quite sure how it all passed, what they talked about. Never anything very serious. The world, politics, other people—all seemed to pass them by. In what she called his highline home, they lived literally in the clouds.

Just occasionally, she felt she would have liked a little more practicality, as, for instance, now. But as he knew that her marriage was not happy, she supposed that, to him, the breaking-up of it was not wrong, but even right. The fact

that she had a child he seemed to ignore. Having no desire
to procreate himself, he was at a loss to understand how
anyone else might want to burden themselves in such a
way. His pictures were his children, "So much more
rewarding and remunerative, Sophie—and one doesn't
have to deal with the same one for so *long*. Think of all that
nappy-changing, all those school fees . . ." And she had
thought, and known that deep down she felt the same way
as he did. Although once one had a child, as she had tried to
explain to him, there were moral obligations, obligations
which, for many years, she herself had tried to fulfil to such
a degree that she had overcompensated out of guilt. How
much of the latter ingredient Alex possessed in his strange
make-up she often wondered. None? A little? Or was it all
there but carefully camouflaged? Because he had made one
tentative suggestion that afternoon which had made her
feel that he was not totally devoid of guilt, or the enormity
of what he had asked her to do. "By the way, you don't
know anyone in the States, do you?" And she had replied,
"No, not really. There's an odd cousin living somewhere
down in New Orleans, I believe." "I see. Forget it. I just
thought it might make things easier for all concerned if you
could have gone away, initially, on a visit. Done the finale
by remote control, as it were . . ."

She closed her eyes. The train gathered momentum after
its last stop. Di da, di da, di da . . . It seemed incredible
that, among all the thoughts going round and round in her
mind, the need to remember that she must collect their
Christmas turkey tomorrow had somehow got amongst
them.

9

"And the beauty of it is," Hugh was saying, "that it's only thirty miles from London and a going concern."

He had by now, it seemed, definitely assumed that it was not just a house they were after, but land, and that land was the best possible place into which his wife's prospective new assets should be sunk.

"That's why I stayed up in town on Friday night. Nipped down to see it this morning before coming on home. You'll love it, Sophie. I'm sure you will. I said I'd bring you over tomorrow. The Hodgsons have asked us both to lunch, incidentally. I thought we could drop Jamie off at Reading. Sorry we can't take him all the way. He's got to join the school party at Victoria by two, hasn't he?"

"Yes."

"Well that's fine then, isn't it? I'll go and telephone the Hodgsons right away."

"Hugh, I . . ."

But he was gone. And anyway she couldn't say anything until Jamie had left. She could hear her son thumping

about overhead, packing. Presently he burst into the room,
tall, broad-shouldered, pink-cheeked. Could this really be
the wan, wheezing child whose bed she had once sat by for
nights on end, holding a vaporizer to his nose, a vomit bowl
to his mouth?

"Mummy, I can't find my old blue sweater."

"Isn't it in your bottom drawer?"

"No."

"I'll come and look in a minute."

"But I want it now. I must get on. I'm going to the
Smithsons this evening, remember. You haven't chucked it
out, have you? You're awfully ruthless sometimes."

"No." So she was ruthless sometimes, was she? God, if
he only knew what she was about to do.

She got up wearily. Hugh still appeared to be telephoning in the other room. He was saying, "I see, and old Sir
Patrick has the shooting rights, does he?"

She found the sweater where she had thought it would
be, tucked away under other clothes at the back of the
drawer. Jamie had evidently not looked very carefully, but
she was glad that he was not so obsessively tidy as his
father. She wondered whether he would really want to go
in for anything as business-like and technical as she knew
farming to be nowadays. He seemed to take much more
after her in many ways. The reports from his art master
were always good. Would he ever, in years to come, forgive
her? Would he, as a grown man, understand? She could
hardly expect him to. She would never be able to explain all
the sex side of it. That was something she could not possibly
do.

The next morning turned out to be cold and clear and blue
and white, the Christmas card kind which usually gave
Sophie great joy, despite a certain regret that they invariably never coincided with the actual event when, as often as
not, it was dull and humid. When she drew the curtains she
was confronted by frosty stalactites dripping from every
branch, a garden which glistened and bristled even though
the sun was, as yet, only palely visible over the tops of the
elms in the opposite meadow. Behind her, in the bathroom,
she could hear Hugh whistling. Across the landing Jamie

was singing, "Don't buy me *lo . . . ove.*" He laid great stress on the last word, carrying it on an inordinate length of time.

She dragged on a dressing-gown and went out into the tiny area leading to Hugh's dressing-room and their joint bathroom.

"Hugh?" She banged on the door of the latter.

The whistling stopped. "Yes, dear?"

"I'm awfully sorry, but I think I may have 'flu. I've hardly slept at all." The last statement was, at least, perfectly true. She had lain awake throughout the night, desperate for an answer to a situation she hadn't bargained for. Why, oh why, had Hugh got on to the Hodgsons' place at a time like this? If only she could see Jamie off. She couldn't, wouldn't, spoil his holiday.

Hugh opened the door. White lather covered the bottom half of his face. For all his fastidiousness and love of gadgets, he had never taken to an electric shaver. His eyes searched hers anxiously. He looked for all the world like a doleful Father Christmas.

"Sophie, are you *sure* . . ?"

"Yes. I'm going back to bed, Hugh. I'm awfully sorry."

"Have you taken your temperature?"

"No. But then you know I never do."

"It could be just a change in the weather. It was awfully cold last night. You might have got a bit chilled, or something . . ." His voice trailed off, lamely, his disappointment blackmailing her, his desire to get her to the Hodgsons at all costs evident with every look and every word. "You might feel better after breakfast. We don't have to leave until, say, ten. Why don't you just go back to bed for a bit?"

Jamie had by now come out of his bedroom on to the landing.

"What's going on?"

"Your mother doesn't feel well. I've told her to go back to bed. See how she feels in an hour or so."

"There's no point in risking pneumonia in order to see a farm in this weather, is there? If you could just put me on the train at Bath, I should have thought it far the most sensible thing to do." Jamie, her son, seventeen, logical, kind, taking her side. She wanted to weep.

He came to say good-bye to her shortly afterwards. He had got his father to agree to putting him on the train at Bath, whether he decided to go on and have lunch with the Hodgsons alone or not. "After all, cars break down sometimes. I can't afford to miss the others."

"No, of course not. Better not come too near me, Jamie. I don't want to pass on anything." In the last few months she was constantly surprising herself at what a skilled liar she had become.

"O.K. But I'm sorry to leave you like this. Hope you'll be better soon."

"I'm sure I will."

"Well, good-bye, then."

"Good-bye. And take care. Try not to break anything."

He was gone. There was a banging of doors, a car starting, a scrunch of gravel, ordinary, everyday sounds. But it was not an every day. It was D-Day or Sophie v Hugh Day, or the Day of *Dénouement*.

10

She was sitting in the drawing-room when Hugh got back at about seven. He had decided to go to the Hodgsons at the last minute because he was still, even without her, anxious to take a second look, something which he would not otherwise have been able to do until the following weekend.

He came in cheerfully, surprised to find her there. "So you're up? Feeling better, I hope?" He went across to the decanter and poured himself a sherry. She had already had two whiskies.

"I was never ill, Hugh."

"What?" He turned and came back across the room. He did not sit down but stood frowning, waiting to be enlightened.

"I said I wasn't ill. I just didn't want to go on to the Hodgsons after seeing Jamie off."

"That's pretty poor, isn't it? I mean, dash it all, Sophie, everything was fixed. You knew how much I wanted you to see the place."

"Yes."

"Then why . . ?"

"Because I'm going to Chicago quite soon, Hugh."

"*Chicago*?" He stood quite still. His eyes never left her face. "Are you feverish or something? If not, please don't talk in riddles. What makes you think you're going to Chicago?"

"Because someone has asked me to go with him."

His frown deepened. Bafflement was total.

"A relative or someone?"

"No. Not a relative. Just someone. Someone I happen to have fallen in love with. And he with me."

"In *love*? Sophie, don't be ridiculous."

Sadly, she realised, as never before, that in the whole of their married life it had never once crossed his mind that another man might admire his wife in any other way than a socially correct and conventional one. Or, indeed, that her own feelings for the opposite sex would be other than platonic. She was still, to him, the cool, calm, copybook Mrs Brent, wife of Hugh, mother of Jamie, an attractive and, on the whole, satisfactory possession.

"Who is this . . . this person? Do I know him?"

"You've seen him once. Many years ago. When Jamie was small. He called at the house and asked to see me when I was out. He'd admired my painting. I seem to recall you described him as 'odd'."

Hugh was obviously having difficulty in remembering. She knew the incident had been completely trivial in his mind.

"Sophie . . . you can't mean . . . not all these years . . . behind my back?"

"No. Not all these years. I happened to meet Alexander Dolan again last summer."

"Last *summer*? My God." He went across to the mantelshelf, put his glass on it and stood there, leaning his head against one arm. He did not speak for several minutes. An ash fell to the grate and he kicked it inwards. She could hear Heidi laying their meal in the dining-room. She felt suspended, caught up in a moment of time which might have been a thousand years.

It was she who eventually broke the silence. "Hugh, I'm

sorry. Terribly sorry. But . . . well . . . you and I . . . It's never been right, has it?"

"It hasn't been all that bad, surely? I've thought, especially since Jamie grew up, that, well, things were better. You seemed happier. Sex isn't everything. I've done my best, Sophie. When I think of some husbands. I've never given you any cause . . ." His voice trailed off. She knew they were treading near dangerous ground. "Does this Dolan man intend to marry you?"

"No."

"No? But if he's asking you to go away with him . . . Sophie, you *can't* be serious."

"I've never been more serious in all my life."

"You mean you want to go away and live in sin with . . ."

She interrupted. "Living in sin is a rather outmoded way of putting it these days, Hugh."

"But what about Jamie? You're not just leaving me, Sophie. You have a son, remember."

"I know." For the first time her voice broke.

Quite suddenly he whipped round and made towards her. There was a look about him she had never seen before, menacing and ugly. His whole face was contorted, his eyes like black pin-heads as he thrust them level with hers. He took hold of each of her arms, pinioning them by his own. Then he began shaking her so violently that her head seemed to rock backwards and forwards like a rag doll's.

"You can't do it, see, you bloody little whore. You've got responsibilities here. I may not have been able to satisfy your excessive sexual appetite, but I've not done you badly, Sophie. You've never wanted for anything else. I've fulfilled my side of the bargain. We've got a good home. Or had, until you fouled it all up. Well, you can bloody well pull yourself together. I'll make allowances. Many men wouldn't. You're probably going through an early change of life or something. You'll get over this madness. I don't believe in divorce. This man's only a passing fancy. You'll see. He'll drop you soon enough when he . . . when he finds another bit of . . . cunt."

He spat out the last word and released her. She heard him leave the room and, for the second time that day, the front door slamming, the car starting up. She wondered idly where he would go, although it did not seem to matter.

Somewhere, in the back of her mind, from that usually tightly-closed box of hers, popped up the cold, unwelcome thought: 'Would Hugh have reacted quite so violently if I were not now the inheritor of such a substantial fortune?' And following quickly after that came another, flashing on to a screen but momentarily, like some caption in a foreign film, dismissed before it had enough time to penetrate, 'Would Alex have asked me to go to Chicago with him if he had not known that I was now financially independent?'

11

"And this," said Lucky brightly, "is an extra bed that comes down from the wall. See?" She pressed a button. A purple, satin-covered bed descended slowly to rest beside the existing double one in what Hugh would have had every justification for calling the "master" bedroom. What with the colour, the noiselessness and the sedateness of the operation, it all seemed somehow macabre, like a cremation service gone into reverse, with the coffin insisting on appearing rather than disappearing into its customary aperture.

"We never *know*, you see," Lucky gabbled on, happily, "who likes what. I mean, some of our guests"—she gave Sophie an arch look—"like to, well, double up together. Some don't. I should say you and your husband will have no need for this one." She pressed the button again, and this time the single bed really did behave almost as Olivia's coffin had done not so very many months ago. As it finally slid into place, Lucky said, "I can see you're vurry happily married."

Sophie swallowed. "Thank you. You've been most kind. You seem to have thought of everything." She did not mean to make a remark that sounded cynical. The words just slipped out. But fortunately any innuendo was lost on Lucky. Her brightness, Sophie guessed, was limited simply to an outward show of startling, almost blinding iridescence. Though small and petite, it would have been impossible to miss Lucky in a crowd. With her luminous make-up, her bouffant, blonde and seemingly plastic hairdo, her scarlet suit with its nipped-in waist but wide, plunging V-neckline revealing, beneath a diaphanous white blouse, the ballooning contours of her over-developed breasts, she seemed like some flashing neon sign, teetering about on her four-inch heels as she extolled the virtues of the Bradley J. Stevens's guest house.

When she had eventually exhausted her tour of instruction, had shown Sophie every labour-saving gadget, had explained the distinctive features of the new waste-disposal apparatus, had opened the door of the huge, unbelievably well-stocked deep freeze and pointed out a confusing amount of switches for either expelling or admitting air or raising and lowering the temperature, she brought her visitor firmly back into the sitting-room with, "Now, how's about you and me having ourselves a little drink? Bourbon?"

Sophie looked at her watch. It was not quite eleven a.m. "I don't think . . . it's a bit early for me, I'm afraid. Thank you all the same."

"Aw, shucks. Do you good. You must be suffering from jet lag. Best thing for you to do, and that cute husband of yours when he gets back from the house with Brad, is to have a couple of stiff ones, then something to eat and get into that nice double bed together and sleep everything off. That's the advice I give all our friends who've just flown in. Marie-Louise—that's the black girl I told you about—will be down shortly to see to your meal. You'll love her. She'll wait on you hand and foot. Get your breakfast if you want, but I guess you'd sooner suit yourselves when you have that. There's coffee, tea, ham, eggs, the lot, in the kitchen. Most

nights I hope you'll dine with us. But if we're out, Marie will
come back and do your dinner as well."

"It's terribly kind of you." In fascinated horror Sophie
watched Lucky go over to what was evidently her *pièce de
résistance*, a small hitherto concealed bar and, ice tongues at
the ready between her scarlet-nailed fingers, utter what
was soon to become an almost stock question, "On the
rocks?"

Having passed Sophie a strong, unwanted drink, she
settled herself down in one of the royal blue tweedily-
covered chairs and looking, in her red and white ensemble,
almost as if she were part of the union jack, continued
confidingly, "You know, Sophie, I'm gonna enjoy having
you two here. I don't mind telling you. I get a bit lonely
sometimes. Brad's thirty-five years older than I am. Did you
know? Think of that. I'm his second wife, but he's my third
husband. I married straight out of High School. Didn't
work, of course. What could you expect? We were both
babies. I was divorced at twenty-one. Then I married a real
whiz-kid. He sure seemed to be going places. Did we
have ourselves a ball! And then . . . I don't know, it all went
wrong. He started going to pieces. Couldn't keep it up.
Began to lose money. Gambled to get it back. I had to watch
him like a hawk. But it didn't do any good. He's inside now.
I managed to divorce him, but he left me stony. No
alimony. Nothing. Can you imagine? Thank God I never
had any children. Of course, marrying so young I'd never
been trained for a job. I didn't want to go back to my old Pa
in Dallas. God, how I hate that place. And then, would
you believe it? Brad came along. An old girl-friend had me
to stay and he happened to come to the house. He'd just
been widowed and, boy, did we need each other. He wor-
ships me, you know. I've got someone who really looks
after me this time. But I do my bit, too. I've made him a good
wife, Sophie. He says the house has never run so smooth.
That's what made him suddenly think about having my
picture painted. And then, afterwards, how nice it would
be to have his family done, too. I expect your husband has
painted you lots of times, hasn't he?"

"No, just once."

"Say! But I expect it's good. Has it ever been on exhibit anywhere?"

"It may be, I think, at this year's Royal Academy." When she had decided to come away with him, there seemed no reason to object.

"Gee . . . isn't that something. It must be wunnerful being married to man like Alex. You don't mind if I call him that, do you? I mean we're all gonna get to know each other pretty well soon, so we might as well start right away with Christian names. I wonder where the hell these two have got to? Just like Brad to want to show Alex something and send us on ahead."

Lucky sighed. The liquid in her glass had diminished at an astonishing rate.

"Of course, the thing I do miss now, Sophie, is sex. I don't mind telling you. Since Brad's heart attack, the doctors have advised against it. Sad." She swilled the remains of her glass round and round. "Would you believe it but, in spite of his age, before his coronary he was a wizard between the sheets. Older men often are, of course. I expect you find that. I don't know how much older Alex is than you, but he still looks kinda vurry virile." To Sophie's barely-concealed relief, the front door suddenly opened and Brad and Alex returned.

When they had at last got rid of their host and hostess, when an indulgent and attentive Brad had helped Lucky into a mink coat and had stooped to attend to the business of seeing her out of her high heels and into thigh-length puce-coloured boots for their short journey home by car, and a beaming Marie-Louise had produced a large, delicious meal to which neither of them could do justice, they did, in fact, take Lucky's advice and go to bed.

"And what," said Alex, light-heartedly, did you and that little man-eater talk about?"

"Her, mostly. And then you."

"Really?"

"In fact, after she had gone into all the gadgets here, we were 'into' sex, as I believe they say, in a big way. She thinks you are 'vurry virile'."

He laughed, lazily and indulgently. "We'd better prove

that, hadn't we?"

He turned towards her. Jet lag or no jet lag, they certainly seemed candidates for the Bradley Js' double bed.

12

The air-mail letters began to appear about five days after Sophie and Alex arrived in America. They were addressed, 'Alexander Dolan Esq.' in mauvish ink by an obviously female hand. Marie-Louise brought them down with her around ten o'clock, by which time the intended recipient had usually left for "the house", as everyone seemed to call the Bradley Js' mansion.

It was impossible for Sophie to ignore them. They all bore a Penzance postmark. She placed them on top of Alex's other mail and left the whole pile on the fake Chippendale table in the hall, where he could hardly fail to see it as soon as he got back. He appeared to be singularly uninterested in his letters, yet she began to feel his casualness was too studied. She became acutely conscious of the way he slid them all into his pocket *en passant* to be read, presumably, later on in private. She herself had received, as yet, little post, other than a few business communications, forwarded according to instructions she had left with certain individuals in England, and an occasional missive sent from one or two loyal girl-friends.

Her departure and final communication with Hugh had been harrowing. She had seen him but once since she had first told him of her intentions, although he had written her several long, reasoned and, in some instances, pathetic letters. After his savage outburst that night, he had driven straight to London, where he had elected to remain at his club until she came, as he put it hopefully, "to her senses".

In the days which followed she had found the sheer physical act of packing, the difficulty of explaining the situation to Heidi ("Can you come into the sitting-room a minute, Heidi?" "Is it important, Mrs Brent? I would like to get the washing on first"), the necessity for making arrangements with her bank and seeing Mr Bellinger, Olivia's solicitor, far more exhausting and embarrassing than she had envisaged. The interview with the latter, someone who had known her since childhood, proved almost as bad as facing Hugh. "Are you *sure*, Sophie, you know what you're doing?" Mr Bellinger had said. "Quite sure," she had replied. She remembered him sighing, everything about him grey and grave and reproachful. "It's a big step, Sophie . . . your mother . . ." "Olivia is dead, Mr Bellinger." And anyway, how much would she have minded, apart from the scandal side of it? She had never liked Hugh.

Sophie kept telling herself that it was important to remain calm and matter-of-fact, rather like keeping one's head in an accident. When she came to think about it, a marital break-up *was* rather like an accident, one that she had sometimes considered possible, occasionally even probable, yet always, in the end, avoidable. But then, suddenly, it wasn't avoidable any longer. Bradley J. Stevens had seen to that. Alex was going away and nothing was going to stop her going with him.

But wanting "out" and getting out were two very different things, as she began to realise only too well. Decisions on seemingly trivial matters assumed alarming proportions: What shall I take? Will I need that summer outfit if we stay on? What shall I do with the rest? What about my personal nick-nacks? Photographs? Jamie's photographs?

Jamie's portrait? Jamie.

In the end she had written her son a letter. It had taken all
of forty-eight hours. Draft after draft had been relegated to
the waste-paper basket. How could she explain? What
excuse did she have? None. Or none that she could give
him. Ever. And it was no good saying, "Look, because of
you I didn't do this eight years ago". He would probably be
disgusted with her. Disgusted, too, because he felt that she
was too old for this kind of thing. He would never understand. She was well aware that the young looked at life
quite differently now, that sex was free-for-all, that possibly
even Jamie himself . . . But when it came to one's
mother . . . *going off*, just like that. People would probably
say, 'How could she *do* it?' And what seemed to make it
worse was that she knew that, outwardly, she didn't appear
to be the type. It wasn't the sort of thing they would ever
expect of her. But then how could *they* know? How did one
ever know about anyone else, for that matter; and certainly
how could anyone, except the two parties *intimately* concerned, know what went on in a marriage, even one's own
children? One's accusers would need to be constantly there,
sitting on the end of the bed like a gremlin or a researcher for
some sex tome, perhaps, noting every orgasm or failure to
achieve it, jotting down each subsequent satisfied snore.
Why was it that human beings were usually so anxious to
commit themselves, with no training and often precious
little experience, to this joint life for better, for worse until—
or so they obviously initially assumed—death did them
part? No wonder Alex had no time for the institution.
Whatever made them go in for such a curious, barbaric
ritual to kick the thing off, dressing the woman up like a
lamb to the slaughter, an angel wreathed in orange
blossom, hell bent, presumably, on becoming a fallen one
by night time. Of course, that sort of thing didn't apply
nowadays. People lived together long before marriage,
young and old alike. They made sure what they were letting
themselves in for. If only she and Hugh had experimented a
bit . . . They would never have married, of course. There
would never have been that ill-fated wedding which
seemed now to have happened to someone else, yet unfor-

tunately still forever indelibly etched on memory: Olivia's *hat*, that ghastly shiny horseshoe which someone had slung over Hugh's and her entwined arms as they came out of the church. All that confetti, the drive south, that disastrous first night at the Savoy because they couldn't make France that day . . . Both tired, tense, unable to . . .

How different it had been from the first time with Alex. How different, indeed, from the first time, only a few weeks ago, when he and she had arrived in Chicago. No jet-lag had stopped them making love just as soon as they got between Lucky's purple sheets.

Poor Lucky. Or, Sophie supposed, perhaps she ought to say lucky Lucky. She had certainly fallen on those tiny feet of hers in marrying Brad, even though she was, at the moment, somewhat sex-starved. But she was so preposterous, so brash, so unbelievably silly: a caricature of a woman. In the beginning she had come to see Sophie most mornings, dressed in a different outfit almost every time, while Alex was up at "the house" painting Brad. Her astonishing confidences, her apparently limitless capacity for alcohol, her appalling taste and total absorption in herself had made her, initially, a strange and interesting phenomenon. But her society soon palled and when Alex started on Lucky's own portrait, so that she had to sit for him each morning, Sophie was left entirely to her own devices. She was both relieved and lonely. For the first time for many years she found herself without enough to do. Marie-Louise, true to Lucky's glowing predictions, kept the guest-house almost clinically clean, and cooked—or transported—food for them with equal skill and efficiency. The weather was such that Sophie was often obliged to stay indoors, although, for the sake of health and exercise, she tried to walk as far as the Home Farm and back each day which, with its smart buildings and steel-enclosed pens, she found depressing in its lack of atmosphere and total dissimilarity to almost any English counterpart with which she was acquainted. She had, moreover, no friends she could call up, and although she knew she had only to speak the word and a car and chauffeur would be sent to drive her the eighteen miles into Chicago, she felt little desire to explore the city alone, especially in sub-zero temperatures. Besides, she wanted to be back when Alex returned for lunch, usually around one-thirty.

What she often felt she would like to do would be to paint and she had broached the subject once or twice to Alex. "Good idea, my love. We'll go to town and get you all fixed up with some materials. What'll you paint?" "You. But I don't suppose there's time for you sit at the moment." "Not really. Perhaps when we get back to England . . ." And there, somehow, the subject had seemed to rest. Their shopping expedition was postponed into an ever-receding Tuesday or Thursday or "when I've done Bradley Junior the First". She sensed that, in some way, he would prefer not to have his "wife" dabbling about with a paint-box or palette while he, the professional, was at work on the main purpose of their visit.

She had not bothered him again and sometimes she felt it was as well. For although he had once referred to her, on the strength of her portrait of Jamie, as having genius, she knew that because she had allowed any talent which she might or might not have possessed to lie dormant for so long, she would, without definite encouragement, find it nerve-racking, even frightening, to bring whatever she did have out of hiding again. And anyway, where could she find a suitable corner in which to paint in their present establishment? Lucky's purple, dirt-free, deodorized, disinfected guest-rooms made an excellent excuse for inaction. She would leave it alone. She had all she wanted, hadn't she? She had Alex.

She looked at her watch. He would be home in an hour or so. There was just time for her to walk perhaps halfway to the farm and back. She went out into the hall and put on her big suede coat and boots. A pity that there was another of those curious letters from Cornwall again this morning, the only communication for either of them . . .

She was surprised to find it had gone from the hall table when she returned. She found Alex in the sitting-room having obviously just been reading it for, as she bent to give him a light kiss, she saw the open envelope sticking from his pocket.

"Back early today?"

"Yes. Bradley Junior's got 'flu."

"Oh, so you couldn't do any work?"

"Not much. Made a few sketches. Lucky brought out the photograph album of all the grandchildren. I must say there's more of the little devils than I thought. By the way, they'd like us to go up to the house early tonight. Brad's bringing his doctor and wife back with him when he returns from Chicago this afternoon."

"Oh. Wasn't he there this morning?"

"No. Had to go off early for his check-up at the hospital."

13

Jealousy was an emotion with which Sophie was little acquainted. During her married life there had never been any occasion for it. Hugh, if not exactly sexless, seemed sexually indifferent as far as other women were concerned. Now, doubts and suspicions attacked her with a ferocity she was powerless to combat. She tried to take a grip on herself, aware that it was probably ridiculous.

She really had nothing to go on. The whole thing was so nebulous. She did not even know whether her uneasiness had more to do with Lucky or the mysterious sender of the air-mail letters from Cornwall. Did she really suppose that Alex, an intelligent, sophisticated man of the world, would ever allow himself, even momentarily, to be attracted to such a brash, small-time, empty-headed little woman as Lucky? Had he not himself referred to her as a man-eater?

She watched Lucky at dinner that night turning all her batteries, full-strength, on to Dr McCutcheon, flashing him with her false-eyelashed eyes, buzzing him with her harsh, corn-craker voice. Occasionally, when the doctor was

allowed a moment's respite, he turned his attention to
Sophie who was sitting on his other side, and asked her
gravely and courteously about England and the various
places where he had been stationed during the war. She
began to feel wretched, a shameless poseur, as she
answered his sincere and intelligent questions, invariably
prefaced by, "Now, tell me, Mrs Dolan . . ." She became
evasive, impersonal, "Yes, she knew the area quite
well . . . Yes, she believed that there had been a large,
underground arsenal there . . . Yes, she often travelled
through Salisbury, the Cathedral was the most beautiful of
all . . . her favourite also . . . infinitely preferable to
Wells . . . Her family? . . . She had one son"—she hesitated slightly at this point—"by a previous marriage." She
had agreed with Alex that, if questioned, she would have to
admit to being his second "wife", but although Lucky had
elicited such information early on, she had been so taken up
with recounting her own life story that any reference to
Sophie's own, unless directly connected with Alex, seemed
to pass her by. She hoped Dr McCutcheon would not make
further enquiries about Jamie and was relieved, although
only momentarily, when, possibly sensing her discomfiture, he switched from asking her about herself and said,
"My wife and I hope to come over to the old country this
fall. We've been planning the trip for some little time."

She knew at once what she ought to say, what would be
the reaction expected of her, what, indeed, she would have
expected herself. She reached for her glass. She must not,
could not, fail him. "You must come and see us . . . you
will let me know, won't you?" What must he be visualizing?
A country home? Hardly Alex's untidy, run-down London
one. A visit to Tremarthen would be best. Surely she would
have been taken there by then?

Later that night, when they were in bed, Alex said, "I
liked those McCutcheons," and she had replied, "Yes,
they're coming to England in the autumn. They're hoping to
visit us." "So his wife was telling me. I managed to head her
off that one, though." "Oh, how?" "Said that, unfortunately, we'd be in the Algarve." "The Algarve? But will
we?" "My dear Sophie, I have no intention of going to the

Algarve. But you have to watch out. If one isn't careful, these Americans, nice as they are, could devour one. I'm a working man, remember."

Not for the first time she marvelled at the way he was able to anticipate and deal with any situation that might arise. Even the trickiest never seemed to ruffle him. Where she would have worried, he merely laughed; where she saw difficulties, he simply saw an easy way out. He had an almost uncanny way of turning any question which he did not want to answer, sometimes even by as little a remark as, "Darling, do you mind if I shut the window?" Just occasionally she felt that there was something troubling him, that his usual spontaneity and love of life had deserted him, and he, sensing that she herself had sensed this, would become especially attentive, especially loving.

She wondered whether it was something like this which had prompted his plans for their short holiday which he announced a few weeks later. "Brad and Lucky are going down to St. Louis for a few days. Going to stay with their daughter and then bring the grandchildren back with them. Thought I'd paint the three little brats together. One fell swoop. I'd like to get everything wrapped up here soon. Brad's offered to lend me the station wagon and I thought you and I would have a breather too. You've been cooped up long enough. You ought to see something of America while you're here. They've recommended some holiday place called The Woodlanders about two hundred miles north near Green Bay."

She was suddenly and wildly elated. He had the power to make her "high" on no other drug but his own magnetism, his special way of treating her. She realised this would be the first time that they would have been away together without him actually working. She could hardly wait.

They arrived at their destination one Friday evening after a long but unhurried journey. Unlike Hugh, who always wanted to get everywhere in the shortest possible time, overtaking everything en route, Alex was a most competent and relaxed driver, wanting, as far as possible, to avoid the motorways. He had been, that day, at his most amusing, most expansive, insisting that Hob be brought out of his holdall so that he could admire the scenery, too.

The Woodlanders proved to be all that Brad had led them to believe. Incredibly, there was even an open fire in their private sitting-room by which, after dinner on their first night, they sat, Alex in one of the deep armchairs, she on the floor leaning against his legs with one of his hands resting lightly on her shoulder. Nothing could have surprised her more than the question which, after a long and peaceful silence, he suddenly asked her.

"Sophie, my sweet, you're not still jealous of Lucky, are you?"

Totally taken aback, she floundered. "I . . . what makes you think I ever was?"

"You haven't been you for several weeks now. Is it her or those damn letters from England?"

So he had noticed. All along.

"Both, I suppose. I'm sorry, Alex."

He sighed. "Sophie, I may be all sorts of a cad, weak where women are concerned, easily led astray, but if there's one woman you need never bother about, it's Lucky. She appals me. She's one of those ones I joked about, remember, when I asked you to come and protect me. Only worse than I've ever known. Oh, she *tried* all right. Bringing out those photograph albums on the day we were alone was as cunning a bit strategy as her bird brain can manage. You know, getting me to sit down on the sofa beside her while she showed them to me, still in her housecoat with all the top and bottom buttons undone showing a great deal more than just the photographs. Actually, the photographs could have been jolly useful. But after seeing a few I made the excuse that I had to get back. That's why I was home early."

"I see." She hated herself. How despicable could one get.

"Since when Lucky has been silently furious. Shouldn't wonder if she doesn't get Brad to cut short my assignment. I wouldn't mind, would you?"

"No." Relief flooded through her like some fast-acting tranquillizer. Then she felt his grip on her shoulder tighten. "There's something else I'd like to say, my sweet. When we get back to England, would you like to come down to Cornwall with me?"

The room seemed very still. With her face turned towards the fire, it was easy to hide emotion. "Yes Alex, I'd like that very much."

He did not speak again for some time and when he did, it was slowly, choosing his words with deliberation and care. "I should have told you before, I suppose. I give you full marks for not pressing me. I . . . just didn't want to spoil anything. And my past is my own problem, Sophie, not yours. When I'm with you I like to live in the present."

She waited. The present seemed to be so very much with them, the fact that they were here, now, in this unexpected Woodlander place, enclosed together in this firelit room, her body against his, the feel of his hand on her shoulder making her whole being alive with response. This was all that mattered, surely? What he was about to say to her would make no difference, whatever it was.

He told his story simply and shortly. She was too much in love to appreciate that she was hearing but one side. He had apparently married, rather hastily and in his late thirties, a French woman called Martina whom he had met in England during the war. He had been an army colonel holding quite an important job connected with camouflage. The fact that he would almost certainly be called upon to take part in the Second Front precipitated the marriage. When peace came his wife was anxious that he should return with her to the Dordogne where her family still lived. He had resisted this because he wanted, as far as possible, to reside and work in the country of his birth for which, as he pointed out, he felt he had helped to fight. This clash of desires and interests led to an unsatisfactory existence, Martina coming over to England for a few months at a time, attending private views, exhibitions and enjoying a more hectic social life than he would have wished, while he, occasionally, made a reciprocal visit to France and stayed with her and her impoverished, ageing parents. After a few such years, during which both went their separate ways and Martina appeared perfectly content with such an arrangement, Alex began a very much more serious affair than usual with an actress with whom he had fallen passionately in love. Not surprisingly, perhaps, Cara, as she was called, wanted this liaison to be regularized by marriage and actually became divorced in order for this to come about. For all her capricious and occasionally outlandish behaviour, she was, at heart, far keener to marry him and, he suspected, bear his children than carry on acting. Eventually, under pressure, he agreed to write to Martina, asking for a divorce also. He had expected problems—for one thing, his wife was a Catholic—but he was by no means prepared for the hysterical outburst on the telephone from France and the news that Martina was leaving for England by car *at once*, and would be with him the following afternoon.

Alex paused in his narrative at this point and then, with effort, continued, flatly, "She crashed, just outside Limoges. Head on. She lost the use of her lower limbs. It meant a wheel-chair. For life."

There was silence in the room now, silence which went on for so long that Sophie wondered if he had forgotten her, if he was simply somewhere back in time, reliving the whole appalling tragedy. Presently, she said, gently, "And Cara?"

"Cara accepted the situation, initially. Or seemed to. I mean, divorce was obviously now out of the question. She asked if she could use my home in Cornwall just to get away from everything. I had to go to France, naturally. When I got back and was at last able to go down and see her, she was quite different. I can't explain it. She had been so vivacious, so beautiful. And now, she'd scraped her hair back, no make-up, no nothing. When I remarked on this she chided me for not having come sooner. I begged her to return with me to London, carry on with her career, but she refused. In any case," he paused uncertainly, as if he had come to a difficult part, "she said her looks had gone, that life had become too much for her. I don't think she ever felt all that guilty about Martina. She'd always hated her, or rather, hated my feelings towards her. She simply said that she was going to give up acting and buy herself a cottage further along the cliffs. She said she would always love me, would look after me whenever I came down, which she hoped would be often. Nothing I could do or say would dissuade her from her plans. She's lived there, ever since, a semi-recluse. Our relationship became entirely platonic, although strangely demanding on her side. She must have guessed there were others. I'm no monk, Sophie. No saint. But she doesn't ask and I don't tell her."

"And your wife?"

"She's still in the family home. Her parents are dead. She's looked after by an elderly retainer."

"Do you see her?"

"I try, now and then. It's never a success. I think she prefers me to stay away. I simply provide financial support."

It was quite dark in the room now. The fire was almost dead. He had finished his story, but there was something she didn't quite understand.

"Alex. You asked me if I would like to come down to Cornwall when we get back. What about Cara?"

"She goes, each summer, to stay with her brother in Scotland for a few weeks. It's the only time she ever leaves the place."

Was there no solution? No escape from subterfuge? Would being with Alex always mean deceit, a hole in the corner existence? She knew she ought to feel pity for these two women. She felt nothing but anger. As for Alex himself, she only felt a need: a need to be with him, a need to be needed and the intenseness of a mutual delight which took but little arousing. A touch, perhaps, or a word or two, such as the ones he was using now, "Sophie, with you it's always been quite different. You're like no other woman I've ever met. You're what I've been looking for all my life . . . Don't you think it's time we went to bed, my sweet?" He pulled her to her feet. "Enough seriousness for one night . . ." He began making love to her as if for the very first time.

14

They returned to England just in time for the Summer Exhibition at the Academy. Alex's portrait of her, called simply *Sophie*, aroused more than a little interest. She found herself confusingly ambivalent about it all. At one time she had wanted to see it hung there. At others, she was scared. It seemed somehow like laying down the gauntlet, announcing her new and present role in society. She mentioned as much to Alex.

"But look, my love, I've painted plenty of other women. It doesn't necessarily mean that I've lived with them all."

"My friends will know."

"But they know anyway, now."

"Yes. But all the same . . . perhaps it would be better if I didn't actually come to the Private View with you."

"As you wish." Did she sense a certain irritation, or perhaps relief in his voice? At the last moment she decided not to accompany him. She knew that there was little likelihood of meeting Hugh, that his interests did not embrace the arts, but there were one or two other people who could,

conceivably, be there and whom she did not want, as yet, to
see.

So far she had met virtually none of Alex's friends. Now,
back in England, she realised a great deal of adjustment
would be needed. She would have to put a brazen face on
things, pretend she did not mind the situation when, in
fact, deep down, she minded very much. It was not as if she
had been abandoned by a husband and was consoling
herself by another liaison. Such circumstances were more
easily understood. But it was she who had left husband,
home and child to become a mistress, and however she
looked at it, whatever way she thought about it, the word
upset her. It might be the permissive second half of the
twentieth century but to Sophie 'mistress' still carried a
stigma; she wished there was a less ugly term which could
be used in connection with a relationship which, as far as
she was concerned, was quite the opposite. And it wasn't as
if she could live with Alex in any other way. After what he
had told her that night at the Woodlanders, that was abun-
dantly clear. She knew there was no possibility of their
marrying. It was not just a question of one other woman,
but two.

She was annoyed with herself for feeling as she did, for
letting her emotions swing about so rapidly and unreliably.
After all, hadn't she herself often railed inwardly against
the institution of marriage? She had longed to break free
many times. Well, she had done it now. If the other side of
the fence was occasionally not quite as she had imagined,
she had no one else to blame. It was worth it, every time. It
was just that, as with so many experiences, the actuality
was different from the concept.

For instance, she hadn't reckoned on the number of
formal and informal invitations Alex might receive which
obviously did not and could not include her. They arrived
almost daily, someone or some Body or other requesting the
pleasure of the company of "Mr Alexander Dolan" at such
and such a function. The less formal ones simply read, "Dear
Alex," sometimes "Darling Alex," and then might carry on,
"We're having a small dinner party on the 30th . . ." or
perhaps, "Alex Dearest, could we possibly winkle you

away from your paint brush to spend a weekend with us in
Shropshire . . ."

She was aware that he considered each invitation carefully. For one thing, many would have interfered with his
work. And to give him credit, he refused to attend any
informal ones unless he asked to take Sophie along with
him, saying, "We've got to let people get used to us, my
sweet. Soon they'll simply accept you as the status quo."
And she would look forward to the occasion, yet with
apprehension, wondering what Desmond and Deirdre or
Fran and Peter would be like and, what seemed more
important, what they would think of her.

When she and Alex began giving reciprocal little parties,
she became more herself. She went to infinite trouble,
taking almost all of two days to prepare a special dinner.
She was a good cook but had allowed herself to get out of
practice, especially towards the latter part of her marriage,
when Heidi had taken over so much. She felt her present
entertaining was successful, that she was liked and
accepted, yet still an object for speculation. The thing which
perhaps pleased her most was that Alex himself was so
appreciative of her efforts.

"I didn't know," he said after one such occasion, "that
you were quite such a domesticated person. Turning out all
those dishes. In fact, I think I shall start calling you Dishy.
You're the best one of all."

She laughed. "You forget. I ran a home, quite well I
think, for many years."

"I suppose so. But you seemed so wrong in that set-up,
somehow."

Since they had returned she had, in fact, done much in
the way of straightening out many of Alex's untidy, ramshackle rooms. He occupied the top half only of a large
house belonging to a retired couple who themselves lived in
the bottom. It was not an ideal arrangement but his enormous studio in the sky was so exceptional that, for him, it
was worth all the other inconveniences, such as sharing and
climbing the wide stone stairs and taking down the rubbish
which he allowed to pile up alarmingly in unlikely corners.
A small, sharp-featured, unhealthy-looking woman called

Mrs Tuffnell came to clean for him three times a week and do his shopping, but before Sophie actually moved in he appeared to have led a hopelessly disorganised and unsatisfactory existence. She wondered how long this had been the case. He had not spelled it out in so many words but she knew she had predecessors. The thought was unwelcome, offensive. She pushed it aside.

What was worrying her more at the moment, and which she could not ignore any longer, was Jamie. She wanted to see him desperately and had said as much to Alex. She had received one stilted letter from her son in reply to her initial one, which had given her so many heart-searchings to write. She knew that it had been cowardly to behave as she had before leaving but, right at the end, she had been afraid that just by seeing Jamie she might have altered course. She had written again several times from America and occasionally received a polite, withdrawn little note in answer, which might have come from a stranger. She gathered that Hugh had bought a house at Sunningdale and that Heidi had left, that Jamie himself was well and working hard for his exams. Such information took up but one side of a sheet of writing-paper.

She waited until she knew his exams would be over and then wrote asking him if he would like her to come and see him or, alternatively, whether he would care to come up to London. She was determined that they should meet before she and Alex went to Cornwall, a visit which was still promised, but which seemed to be constantly postponed into an ever-receding week or month. She understood now that Cara would not be going away until August.

Jamie elected to spend a Thursday with her in London at the end of term. He said that it would work quite well, as he had arranged to spend the night with a school friend with whom he was proposing to go to France the following day. It occurred to her how nice it would have been if she herself had been able to ask him to stay. But it was only a fleeting, fanciful idea. For one thing, Alex would certainly not have approved. Having no paternal feelings himself, he either could not, or would not, recognise any in her. But there was another reason why such a desire was out of the question.

She knew that she would be quite incapable of saying, "Good night, Darling," to Jamie, and then withdrawing into another bedroom with a lover. It was better to keep him right away from the establishment. Take him to a show. Give him an expensive lunch.

When she told Alex what she had planned he merely nodded and said, "Pity it's that day, because I've just got this invitation for us both from Vincent Matheson, or rather I suppose he's got the hospital to send it. They're giving that luncheon they promised in his honour, as soon as my portrait of him was finished."

"Oh." She was suddenly sick at heart. She liked Vincent. He was a prominent surgeon, about to retire, somewhat on the young side. "I don't believe in waiting until one has to go," he had once remarked. "Better to pack it in while they still want you to stay." The hospital for which he worked had commissioned Alex to paint his portrait and for the last few weeks Vincent had been coming to the house regularly at eight thirty each morning, which was the only time he could spare for sittings. That someone, not from the artistic world, had obviously liked and been exceptionally kind to her, meant a great deal. She had been looking forward to the luncheon which Vincent had hoped they would both attend. It would have been the first formal one at which she would have accompanied Alex.

"Better put your son off, Dishy. You can see him some other time."

"No. He's coming straight from school and then leaving for France the next day."

Alex frowned. "As you wish." He was reacting in exactly the same way as he had when she told him that she would not be accompanying him to the Private View at the Royal Academy. With an effort, she added, "I'd like to alter it, Alex. I really would. But I don't see how I can." He appeared to be concentrating on something in the daily paper.

She met Jamie at Waterloo on the appointed day and took him to lunch at Simpsons. He seemed taller and thinner. The boyishness in his face had been replaced by some-thing—she couldn't quite define it—slightly wary and

cynical. He kissed her perfunctorily at the station, his whole
manner off-hand, as if he were determined to play their
reunion low-key.

Over the meal he asked her no questions, merely replying, sometimes in monosyllables only, to her own: Yes, the
exams had been pretty awful. He didn't think he had done
all that well, especially in history. If he didn't make univer-
sity, he felt he would just as soon go to an agricultural
college. Farming seemed as good a bet as anything
provided someone could stump up some cash. He knew his
father was keen on the idea. She wondered about his last
remarks, how pointed they were. She asked him how Hugh
was and he hesitated, as if a report on his father needed
some thought. "He's all right," he said, at length. "I haven't
seen him much this term. He's a bit lonely, naturally." As
for the house in Sunningdale, it wasn't "bad", there was
"more to do", there was a "cleaning-woman and someone
who comes in to cook at weekends and so forth, a neigh-
bour's daughter who's done a domestic science
course . . ."

Only at the end of the meal did he become a little more
expansive. She noticed that he had drunk more than his
share of wine. "I'm sorry about . . . what happened . . .
you and Daddy . . . I don't suppose"—it was the first direct
question he had asked her—"you'd think of coming back?"

The noise in the restaurant had reached an uncomfortable
level. It suddenly seemed too hot and she wanted to get
out, quickly. She signalled for the waiter, aware that Jamie's
eyes were watching her carefully. "I'm asking this myself,"
he went on. "I mean Daddy didn't put me up to it or
anything."

"I'm sure you are, Jamie." She leaned down to pick up
her gloves which had slipped to the floor. "It's just . . . I
couldn't . . . Your father and I . . . weren't really right
together."

He nodded. He did not seem surprised. "I know. Plenty
of other people's parents have divorced. Shall you, do you
think?"

"I don't know, at the moment. It would be more satisfactory, I feel. Altogether cleaner somehow. Perhaps your

father may have changed his mind. He was against the idea
six months ago. I shall have to ask him."

"Then you could marry this Dolan chap."

"No."

"Oh." He did not pursue the matter further. She paid the
bill and they left for the theatre.

Later, when she dropped him off in a taxi at his friend's
house in Chelsea, he said, "Thanks for the day. See you
again soon." And she turned away, hoping he had not
noticed the tears which had long been close to the surface
and which now spilled over, blurring the sight of him
walking up some front steps to ring a bell.

She could hear Alex singing, lustily, when she got back to
the house: "Night and Day, you are the *one* . . ."

He broke off as she entered the studio. "Hello Dishy. You
missed a splendid luncheon. Done your little mother act?"

Without a word, she turned and left him alone.

15

"I'm sorry, Dishy. But you did once tell me that you never wanted a child."

She went on slicing a tomato with studied attention. It was the first time that she had ever shown him anger. He perched on one end of the kitchen table, picking up one of the slices and putting it in his mouth. She was surprised, somewhat mollified, that he had bothered to come and look for her.

Presently she said, "Even if you don't want a child, it's different when you've got one. You're . . . responsible for it."

"But Jamie's almost a grown man now. He's not your responsibility any more. In his youth I should have said that you'd done more than your share."

"It may be one way of looking at it. But one goes on feeling responsible somehow. And I've let him down. I know he feels that. I'd like to make up. I may have failed in one way. But I could help in others."

"Such as?"

"Financially. I think he may want to farm."

"But he's only eighteen. Surely you're not suggesting buying a lad of eighteen a farm, are you?"

"Of course not. I meant, later on, if that's what he wants to do and has done the necessary training. I could, at least, go some way towards getting him started." She moved about the kitchen fetching vinegar and olive oil, preparatory to mixing a salad dressing, aware that her statement had surprised Alex, that he was giving it more than a little thought.

After a while, he said, "You could ruin him, you know. The young don't necessarily need, or want . . . to be spoon fed. No one ever gave me a cent."

"I *know*, Alex. It's just, well, I don't want him to think I've completely abandoned him. And if I've got the money . . ."

"But have you?"

"I still don't know, exactly. Bellinger's taking his time. Olivia's affairs were complicated. The estate isn't by any means wound up."

She wished they hadn't got on to the subject. There was often constraint between them about it. She felt that they had arrived at a conversational cross-roads and she didn't know how or which way to go on. To her mortification, she was even beginning to wonder whether it had been a mistake to see Jamie at all. She bent down to look at a veal fricassee in the oven which she had prepared earlier that day and, as she began to extricate it, the whole thing suddenly slipped from her grasp and crashed, loudly and accusingly, on the floor.

"Dishy. Leave it. I'll clear it up later." Within seconds he was round on her side of the table, holding her very firmly. "We are going out. You've had enough today. I'm sorry. I should have realised."

She allowed him, not unwillingly, to lead her into another room where he pushed a drink into her hands. "I'm taking you to Rosini's."

"I'm not all that hungry, Alex."

"Neither am I. But there's no need to hurry. It'll take me quite a time to deal with that disaster in the kitchen." She smiled a little, knowing how helpless he was over anything to do with that particular area.

"Besides, I've something nice to tell you first. As a matter of fact, I was going to do so when you came in. That's why I was singing."

"Oh."

"Cara's fixed her date for going to Scotland. August 15th. And I've been thinking, my love, Cornwall seems the ideal place for you to start painting again. You'd like that, wouldn't you?"

Her spirits lifted. The drink, his news, the thought of painting and, more important, the fact that Alex himself had thought about it and suggested it, seemed to wash away all the anxieties of the day. He fussed around her, cosseting, cherishing, his enthusiasm for the proposed trip turning the evening into an unexpected success.

It was not until a week or so later that he suddenly announced his more detailed plans for going to Cornwall; it was just after he had taken her on a shopping expedition to buy her necessary painting equipment. The latter, he explained, was a pre-holiday present from him, "a kind of thank you for looking after me so well. When we get away I insist we live much more simply. No more Boeuf Stroganoff, no more soufflés. You know, a jug of wine, a loaf of bread and thou . . ."

She was sitting on the floor gloating over his purchases. When he made his next remark she thought perhaps she had not heard him aright. "I'll have to go ahead, my love, if you don't mind. I thought I'd drive down with all our bits and pieces and then you could come on by train a few days later."

She put down the brush she was fingering and stared at him. "Why, Alex?"

"Dishy, surely you must understand. I haven't seen Cara since last Christmas. She was terribly upset when I didn't go down as soon as we got back from America. I've never been quite so long without a visit, but I just didn't want to leave you. I feel I must be there for a little while before she goes off. After all, she's kept an eye on my house all this time. It would be very unkind if I arrived just after she'd left. It would look as if I was purposely avoiding her."

"I see." Did she see? Not really. It was all so odd. She felt out of her depth, sucked into some whirlpool of emotions— both her own and other people's—which left her exhausted, bewildered and totally incapable of resistance. Whatever kind of a woman was this Cara? What sort of hold did she have on Alex? Did he really think that she, Sophie, would not mind? For the second time within less than two weeks their conversation, usually so easy and mutually enjoyable, foundered, as if some elusive, intangible, but at the same time weighty third party was determined to butt in and put a stop to it. She did not know what to do. She longed for help over a situation which seemed beyond her control. For the first time since she had left Hugh a kind of nameless fear took hold of her. It was nothing she could define, simply a desolate emptiness in which she had no autonomy and had lost all sense of direction.

"Dishy." He was suddenly on the floor beside her, his deep penetrating eyes staring into hers, willing her, almost hypnotising her, with his look, his words. "I promise you . . . it's simply an old friendship. I have . . . obligations. You must know you're everything to me now. You mustn't grudge poor Cara what little occasional happiness I can give her."

Put like that, Sophie realised, her attitude seemed petty, unjustifiable and selfish. And wasn't he really a much nicer person than she, refusing to desert an old flame, trying, within limits, to do what he could for her? But then why wasn't he more understanding about Jamie? Or was filial love as beyond his comprehension as hers towards a former lover? Although when she came to think about it, she had no former lovers. Alex was her one and only and, thank God, present one. Was she now going to risk losing him by being unco-operative, mulish? Was she prepared to spoil the happiness of a whole new way of life because he wanted to fulfil a small duty to the past?

Miserably, she looked away, anywhere to be released from these strange, compelling eyes. Then, as if reading her thoughts, she heard him say, softly, "Don't spoil it, Dishy. We have so much. All this, for instance . . ."

Very gently, he began stroking one of her legs.

16

"So this is the love nest, is it?" Elizabeth Farley leaned back on the enormous sofa in Alex's studio and lit a cigarette. "Very nice, too." She kicked off her shoes, her big ill-co-ordinated frame looking singularly unbecoming in a mustard-coloured dress, yet somehow managing to radiate normality and cheerfulness. She was Sophie's oldest friend. With Elizabeth she was suddenly back in the Lower Fifth.

"I'd never have thought it of you, I must say. But then you always were a bit of a dark horse. What a lark! Where's lover-boy gone?"

"Cornwall. I'm meant to be going down on Saturday. I must say it was jolly good of you to come at such short notice."

"My dear, I couldn't wait. I haven't seen you in ages. It does George and me no end of good to see the back of each other occasionally. Five days will give him just enough time to miss me. I shall return with my horizons broadened by the big city and some pâté de foie gras from Harrods in a plastic bag. What could be more delectable. I may even have a facial. Go back to Little Biddingford with a veneer of sophistication. The trouble is one go at the garden or a session with the washing machine and the whole thing rubs off. Wish I had your face and figure. D'you know, Sophie, you're looking more gorgeous than ever. A bit tense, perhaps, but it suits you. Fine-drawn. I think that's the right expression. As if you're living life. There's a kind of *femme fatale* look about you. Tell me, what's it like?"

"What's what like?"

"You know. Kicking over the traces. Living in sin, as they used to say, only they don't any more, except for the inhabitants of Little Biddingford. I must say, we are a stuffy lot. Sometimes I feel I want to shock them, just for the hell of it. Only I can't imagine leaving Goerge."

"Of course not. You and he are a fixture. How is he, by the way?"

"All right. Dedicated to his orchids and his bees and the parish council."

"And to you, needless to say."

"I expect so. I'm just lucky, I suppose. We've had our differences, but we don't get worked up easily. Sometimes I feel we don't *mind* enough about things. We just jog along in double harness. I never thought you and Hugh did, somehow."

"No."

"It was sex, wasn't it? Usually is."

"Yes."

"You never said. Very loyal. And now it's fine, I presume?"

"Yes."

"How super. Are you getting a divorce?"

"Hugh doesn't seem to want one. I suppose, with the changed divorce laws, we might, eventually, on the grounds of living apart."

"Then you could marry lover-boy."

"No. I can't marry lover-boy, as you call him."

"Why not? Can't he get unhitched too?"

"No. There are too many . . . complications."

"Oh God. I hoped life was working out for you at last.

Don't tell me he's going to keep you guessing?"

"No. He's told me there's no question of it. It's an odd
story. I'll tell you sometime. But I think right now we'd
better have something to eat."

"That's fine by me. Even if I have a facial, I'm not going
to keep to my diet while I'm with you. This is a spree."

Sophie began to realise how much she had missed such
an ordinary undemanding relationship. They shopped, did
two theatres and a film, sat in Regent's Park and often
talked far into the night. Elizabeth was resurrecting, hourly,
something which seemed infinitely precious, to which part
of Sophie wanted and needed to cling. She was so totally
reliable and predictable. She gave Sophie the feeling that if
she were to rob a bank or commit a murder, Elizabeth
would arrive with some metaphorical smelling salts and
sort everything out. Why was it that some women were so
well-adjusted, so well-equipped with kind shoulders on
which their weaker sisters could lean, who married the
right partner and went through life indulgent, yet a little
detached from their husband's foibles?

"Of course," Elizabeth said one evening towards the end
of her stay, "sex has never meant all that to me, Sophie. I
guess I could be called cold or something. Perhaps it makes
life easier in a way."

Cold? Elizabeth? She seemed so warm of heart, so understanding and almost uncannily perceptive. "Don't forget,
my dear," she said, standing on the platform just before her
train left, "If ever you want a break or a bolt-hole, Little
Biddingford awaits. No glamour. Not much life, but we'd
love to have you."

"Thanks. I'll remember. But I hope it'll be a break rather
than a bolt-hole."

"Oh, so do I. All the same, Cornish Cara might get you
down sometimes, I feel."

How right she was. Cara did get her down. She found
herself thinking about her more and more on the journey to
Cornwall the following day. The fact that Alex spoke of her
so little, and then with reluctance, made her an object of
added curiosity. Had she, for instance, been staying with
him the last five days? He had once vouchsafed that she

visited his house almost daily during his absence in order to
see everything was all right. When she had asked him if that
was really necessary he had said, "It's pretty isolated, my
sweet. Gales, rain, break-ins. Anything could happen. I'm
very grateful to her." And Sophie had simply replied, "I
see," as she often did, yet did not really see at all. She felt an
unexpected fierce antagonism towards this woman, as if
she were conducting some private warfare against a
nebulous but curiously cunning opponent, who seemed
astonishly adept at remote control.

17

She could hear the surge of the sea from the bedroom in which they lay. She had never made love to the sound of waves before. Was the rhythm, the sighing, the wildness, an aphrodisiac? She could now understand what Alex had meant about his house being isolated. Tremarthen was larger and much more rambling than she had expected, almost a cliff-hanger—she could think of no better word—built by some visionary or hermit, perhaps, although one could never call its present owner that.

"I've missed you so, Dishy." He brought a hand up to her cheek and kissed her very gently. "Tomorrow I'll show you the cove. We'll picnic. Shall you like that? Isn't it strange that we've never picnicked before?"

When she woke he was no longer beside her and, for a moment, she panicked, trying to re-orientate, aware of the crash of water against rocks and then, mercifully, a gentler noise and a welcome aroma: Alex was downstairs getting breakfast.

"There." He put the tray on her lap. Coffee, butter, toast,

marmalade and an assortment of china and eating utensils that would scarcely have been saleable at a jumble stall, yet the novelty of which only seemed to add to the frivolity of the occasion.

He sat on the end of the bed, smiling broadly. "I told you, didn't I, that you weren't to do so much down here. This is *your* party. I'm so *pleased*, my love, that we're here at last, together just where I wanted us to be."

His delight seemed so genuine, his enthusiasm childlike and infectious. At any moment she felt he might produce a bucket and spade.

"How long have you had this place, Alex?"

He paused. "Just after the war, I guess."

She refrained from asking when he had first brought Cara there.

"Do you paint much while you're down here?"

"No, not a lot. I mean, for one thing there aren't the sitters. I think I use it more to recuperate in than anything else. Re-inspire I suppose you might say. With you, it's just about the perfect remedy."

"Will recuperating include sitting for me?"

"Of course. If you want. But I'd like to show you around first. You need a day off today. When you're ready we'll go on a conducted tour."

Later that morning, carrying a picnic, he led the way down the steep cliff path while she followed with their bathing things. She was surprised to discover how much care and thought he had put into shopping in her honour: a lobster purchased from a local fisherman, salad, fruit, wine.

"I have a special place where we can hide it all if you'd like to walk along the shore first. What sort of a swimmer are you?"

"Average, I think."

"Ever done much surfing?"

"Not really."

"Just as well. If you're not all that keen we won't bother. It means going to another bay which is much more crowded. The beauty of this one is that it's comparatively unfrequented even at this time of the year. I suppose the inaccessibility saves it. Here, it's better just to bathe, when the tide's right."

They spent almost all day on the beach. Sometimes, for a while, when he was a little away from her, clambering ahead over rocks or going down to the sea for a second bathe, this time alone, she wondered whether he had done the same sort of thing with Cara only a few days before. The thought intruded, unwelcome but persistent. But with his returning presence she was able to push it away. As long as he touched her, held her, all fears dissolved as did her body later that afternoon when he began to make love to her again. She held back, but scarcely for a moment.

"Can we . . . here?"

"Of course. A rock on either side. Only the Statue of Liberty over the horizon. That family with the kids packed up and gone. You don't suppose I chose this spot for nothing, do you?"

In the days which followed she made a big effort to continue simply to live in the present. It was ridiculous to allow the thought of Cara to spoil something which she knew could, so easily, be nearly perfect. She must not, would not, give in to what she feared was becoming almost an obsession. When left to herself—which admittedly was not often—she knew it was stupid to imagine some dis-embodied squatter watching her as she made an omelette, criticising as she made their bed in a haphazard, even slovenly, way which would have horrified her had she still been married to Hugh. But the niggles kept returning. How, for instance, did Cara make beds? Or omelettes? Was she tidy, capable, scatter-brained, thin, fat, sexy? Why, in heaven's name, couldn't Alex *talk* about her?

One day, when the absent woman had occupied her thoughts more than usual, had even interfered with her work on the painting she was attempting, she pleaded a headache, went upstairs and lay, face down, on the bed. She would have to put a stop to these fantasies. There must be some way to exorcize them. She was thinking so hard that she was not aware of Alex until he had come into the room and was standing right beside her.

"Sophie, what is it?"

She sat up with a start. She had known him over a year,

yet it was the first time that she had made a direct request which she knew would be unwelcome.

"Alex, will you take me to see Cara's cottage? I presume you have a key."

He was silent. She knew he had heard her, that he was merely stalling for time. When at last he spoke he did so slowly, choosing his words with deliberate care.

"It would hardly be right, my dear. Besides, would it do any good?"

"I can't stop thinking about her."

"I am aware of that."

"Then why don't you ever refer to her. Bring her out into the open. It would be so much easier. For me."

He sighed and went to the window, staring towards the sea. The day had been grey, a heavy mist blotting out the view, closing in on the house, damp and cloying, trapping them together, making a prison of what, but a short while ago, seemed a pleasure-ground. The whole place had changed and somehow she felt herself to have changed with it. There was a sudden bitter defiance within her, an assertion of will that she hardly knew she possessed.

"Who do you think I am, Alex? Do you expect me not to mind about her? Not to ask questions? Why do you bring me here in this clandestine way? If she doesn't share your life, why can't she meet the person who does? What's the matter with her? With you? It's . . . abnormal . . ." Her voice had risen. Hysteria was in it.

Then he was on top of her, holding her down, pinioning her arms, a wildness in his eyes. "I've told you, you little fool. My relationship with Cara is entirely platonic and has been for a long, long time."

"But that's not perhaps what Cara wants." She seemed to be fighting him now, mentally and physically.

"I don't care what Cara wants." His look was savage. He began tearing at her blouse, tugging at her skirt. "It's only you I want. If this won't prove it, nothing will."

She was scarcely conscious of what time he left her. When she woke it was quite dark. She groped for the light and looked at her watch. 11 p.m. The house seemed silent. Only the sea, its reverberations muted a little by the mist,

echoed dully and persistently somewhere far below. She
got up, dragged on a housecoat and went downstairs.
There was no sign of Alex anywhere. She went into the
kitchen and poured herself a drink, something which had
become more necessary to her of late. Where was he?
Walking the cliffs? Down on the shore? Oh God, not in this
weather. Supposing he slipped? She opened the back door
and stepped outside, shivering in what seemed like the
coldness of a winter's night. She was almost relieved to find
that his car had gone. There was nothing she could do but
sit and wait.

Hunched at the kitchen table, she watched the hands on
his old metal alarm clock creep round to twelve, during
which time she thrice refilled her glass. Fear gave way to
confusion. Perhaps she should dress? Ring the police? How
he would hate that if he were all right. But how long did one
leave a situation like this? They would ask questions. A
lover's tiff? Although hardly, not at the end. They had made
up in perhaps the only way possible for them, by a passion
so strong, so urgent, so irresistible that if only he would
walk in now she would assure him that she would never
mention Cara's name again.

She began to play a childhood game of imagining him on
the way home: now he's at those cross-roads, now he's
turned the corner by the headland, he's got to the narrow
part, he's halfway along the dirt track, he's had to slow for
the bumpy bit, now he's beginning to hurry, he wants to get
back as much as I want him back . . . I can actually hear the
sound of his car . . .

She stood up, swayed a little and held on to the table.
"Alex Darling, Thank God . . ."

"It's not Alex Darling, I'm afraid." A tallish woman
wearing tinted glasses, a white head scarf tied tightly over
her head, stood on the kitchen threshold.

Sophie opened her mouth, the scream in her throat
refusing to come.

"Don't worry, my dear. I shan't hurt you."

"Cara . . ?" The word came out at last.

"Right, first time." She went straight to a cupboard and,
with a proprietary air, picked up a glass. "I think I could do

with a little of what I see you must have had quite a lot of.
I'm sorry Alex is out. But perhaps it's just as well. I shall
have an opportunity of getting to know you a little, alone. I
felt sure you must be here. That's why I cut short my
holiday in order to meet you."

"But, what made you think . . . I mean . . . you don't
know me at all."

"My dear, I don't know you—yet. But I've known *of* you
for a long time."

"You mean . . . Alex has talked to you about me?"

"Of course not. But there's usually someone. I'm not
always sure exactly when they change, but he runs to
pattern. I've been aware you've lasted rather longer than
most. There hasn't been one of his helpless periods for quite
some time. That's why I was intrigued to find out what sort
of a person you were. You're very pretty, although I can see
you must have had rather a bad evening."

Sophie stretched out a hand for the gin bottle and felt
another one hold hers tightly by the wrist. "I shouldn't, if I
were you. It's so easy, when Alex is being difficult. Don't
worry. It isn't the first time he's gone rushing off into the
night."

She looked at the woman across the table, wishing that
she would take off her dark glasses so that she could see her
eyes. She must have been beautiful once. Her face was pale,
skeletal, the skin drawn tight across the high cheekbones.
There seemed something infinitely sad about her, as if she
were possessed of wisdom born out of more than an ordinary share of suffering. Confronted with that look, those half
hidden eyes, Sophie lowered her own, feeling at a disad-
vantage, like a child. She remained silent.

"How much has he told you?"

"Not a lot. I gather you were to have been married if he
had been able to get a divorce."

"Yes and no."

"What do you mean?"

"My dear, Alex has what might be called a 'convenient'
memory."

"I don't understand."

"No? Perhaps not. But he's a little apt to distort the facts.

There was a time, admittedly, when he promised to ask his wife for a divorce in order to marry me, but it was something he was always *going* to do and then never seemed to get around to it. We had several rows and then, finally, one really big one, rather as I imagine you may have had tonight. We were staying down here and he pushed off back to London. I wasn't working at the time—I'd been in a play which had been a terrible flop—so I decided to stay on down here until he made up his mind."

"But he did. I mean, he said he wrote to Martina . . ."

"Oh yes, he wrote, all right, but not for another nine months, during which time someone else came on the scene, an altogether tougher, more designing female. It was not for my benefit that he at last got around to asking for a divorce. She made him do it."

There was silence for several minutes. Sophie noted dully that the hands of the clock were pointing to a quarter to one. She had registered what the woman across the table had said, yet she was incapable of comprehending it or appreciating its implications. There were too many pieces of the puzzle still missing. Presently she said, "What happened to this other woman?"

"Oh, she cleared off after the accident, as soon as she saw there was no future in it for her."

"And you? Why did you decide to live here?"

"I'd had a bad shock, my dear. I was very much in love with him, as you are now. Being jilted affects some women rather more drastically than most. In my case . . ." She broke off, raised both hands, simultaneously whipping off her dark glasses and pushing at her head scarf which slid backwards, together with the hair underneath it.

The woman now confronting Sophie had no eyelashes and was completely bald.

18

Alex telephoned early that morning. Cara had spent the rest of the night at the house, taking herself off into one of the spare rooms. Neither woman had slept and were once again downstairs when he rang. Although both sprang to pick up the receiver, Cara held back just in time, remembering that, officially, she was not supposed to be there.

In contrast to Sophie's high-pitched and peremptory "Hullo?" Alex's voice sounded casual to a maddening degree. "Hullo Dishy. Sorry."

She sat down suddenly, tension giving way to numb relief. "Where . . . are you?"

"London."

There was a long silence. She was vaguely aware of Cara somewhere in the background, watching her from behind her execrable glasses.

"Dishy, I felt it best. I . . . had to get away for a bit. I'll be down again on Saturday."

Still she did not speak.

"We'll go out to dinner. Book at the Fisherman's Arms,

will you?"

"I'd . . . sooner not . . ."

Impatiently, he interrupted. "Dishy, don't be a fool. You must realise. I adore you. It's just that sometimes . . . I mean, you have rather got a bee in your bonnet at the moment, haven't you? Now, be a good girl and do as I say. I'll give you another ring this evening." There was a click and the line went dead.

"I think," said Cara, "that you and I will now have a damn good breakfast. I don't suppose you ate at all last night, did you?"

"I'm not hungry."

"Doesn't matter. You've got to eat something. All that alcohol on an empty stomach. Oh, don't think I haven't been through that stage, too." She busied herself getting butter and eggs out of the refrigerator. "Scrambled, I think. Oh good, I see you've got some bacon. I'll grill a little." Within a few minutes she laid a full plate before Sophie. "For God's sake, eat it. Then I want to talk to you."

To her surprise, Sophie found herself eating everything, rather as a child obeying orders, although she wished her invigilator opposite would remove her glasses, however strange her appearance without them. Yet at the end of the meal, the words which came from behind that deceptive façade seemed straightforward enough.

"Look, my dear. It seems to me, for all your attractiveness, you haven't had much experience of men and you've had the misfortunte to meet up with an exceptionally tricky one. Alex is, in some ways, as selfish as they come, but he has that *je ne sais quoi* as far as women are concerned. I believe you to be still something of a novelty to him. But you've got to face it. He isn't the faithful type. Although he does have one unusually redeeming quality. He will never completely cast off anyone who, as it were, doesn't want to be cast off. That's where I come in. You may think I'm all sorts of a tough woman. I'm not. I still need Alex. In one way, I suppose more so, since this ghastly affliction overtook me. I couldn't get by without his support and friendship. And he honours that. We're still very close, much closer than when we . . ." Her voice stopped, uncertainly, yet her half-hidden gaze still seemed to be directed straight towards Sophie. Presently she got up, made herself another cup of coffee and then, returning to the table, went on, "You may think I'm more selfish than he is, the way I hang on. But Alex is really all I have left. My brother doesn't count for much. In any case, his wife can't stand the sight of me, *literally*." She gave a short, hard laugh as she emphasised the last word, before adding, "I can appreciate that I must have given you all sorts of heartaches."

"Yes. I mean, it's so . . . well . . . unusual."

"But it must have helped, meeting me, hasn't it? I can't be the threat you've been envisaging. More of a drag really. Poor Alex. Deep down he means well, but he can't really cope with the other rebellious, passionate side of his nature."

"What exactly are you trying to tell me?"

"My dear, I'm simply warning you, as an older woman. It's up to you. As long as you can take it, I'm sure you'll carry on. You're obviously very much in love with him. But you must know," she paused, meditating a little before interjecting a few words almost to herself, "no, perhaps you don't" and then continuing, "affairs of the sort Alex engenders can only keep going by a kind of admixture of partings, reconciliations, further rows until one or the other gets exhausted—usually the woman—and then he simply moves on to another sexual partner. You and he seem to have got to the row and parting stage. Then you'll have a lovely time making-up when he comes down at the weekend. This sort of thing could go on quite a time, depending on how much it means to you both, how long you're prepared to play the game. God, you probably won't thank me for sermonizing like this. I'd better be getting back home now. I've said far too much. I'll leave you to sort things out."

For a long time after she had gone Sophie sat on at the kitchen table, laying her head down across folded arms. She knew that what Cara had said made sense. The other woman had simply voiced something which she herself had long been refusing to acknowledge. She also knew that at some point—she was not sure exactly when—she had lost out a little, that there had been a shift in her relationship with Alex, that she was on more uncertain ground, her feet sinking into quicksand from which she was aware that she was too weak, too besotted, to extricate herself. For the first time since she had left Hugh she wondered about the possibility of returning to him.

Evening came and still Alex did not ring. She brought out the gin bottle, puzzled and then alarmed to see that its contents had diminished to such an astonishing extent. She believed that he kept reserves in one of the top cupboards and searched about until she found them. She told herself that he would probably not call until after dinner. Yet where would he be having dinner? Out, somewhere. That was certain. He never dined alone if he could help it. When he did ring she was determined to sound cheerful, matter-of-fact, as if a lover walking out and going back to London in the middle of the night was one of the most natural things in the world, as trivial an incident as he himself had appeared to assume. With her first drink she felt confident that she could carry this off. With her second, she felt positively light-hearted. And after all, it wasn't as if they had really quarrelled, not after what had happened just before he left.

But Alex did not ring. Pride, or what was left of it, prevented her from telephoning him. Besides, she did not want to find him out, however sure she was that he would be. For the second evening in succession she sat at the kitchen table drinking alone. At eleven, fuddled and dispirited, she dragged herself to bed, lay down and, fully dressed, fell swiftly into a heavy, alcohol-induced sleep. Some time later she was violently awakened by a merciless clamouring in her ear. Still stupefied, she tried to remember where she was, what had happened. The previous day seemed blank. Time had gone wrong. It was quite a few moments before she could collect her wits enough to realise that the telephone was demanding to be answered. She felt more perplexed than anything else on hearing Alex's voice.

"Dishy? Sorry to ring at this hour, but I've only just got back."

"Back . . ?"

"Yes. I've been out to dinner. With Vincent Matheson. I

say, are you all right? Your voice sounds odd."

"Does it? . . . I was asleep."

"Oh, my poor Darling. Please forgive me. Only I did promise to ring. I thought you might be worried. Now you go right back off again. Looking forward to Saturday. Mind you book that table."

After several abortive attempts at replacing the receiver, she was still sufficiently anaesthetised not to do anything other than return to sleep, as Alex had advised. When she woke, she wondered, perhaps, whether the sight of Cara, sitting on the end of her bed, was simply all part of some long nightmare. And surely it was not she herself, Sophie Brent, lying there with something akin to a traction engine raging through her head, a mouth like sand-paper and a mind so dulled and hopeless that the sight of her dark-bespectacled uninvited visitor, contemplating her dispassionately like some hunched-up crow, neither surprised, shocked, nor embarrassed her.

"I kept ringing and got no reply. I wondered if you'd gone but thought I ought to look in to make sure. I see you just left the telephone off the hook."

Sophie tried to turn her head and winced. Memory returned, but spasmodically. She must have failed to get the receiver properly back into place after Alex had called. Or had he really telephoned? What had he said? What had she said?

"How long have you been drinking as badly as this?"

"Never. Until now."

"I think I'll go down and make some coffee."

She did not demur. She felt almost grateful to be taken charge of. When Cara reappeared she simply said "Thank you" and accepted the cup which she handed to her.

"I presume Alex never rang?"

"No. Yes, he did . . . sometime in the night. I'm not sure when."

"Typical. Tell me, are you just going to hang on until Saturday or do you want to get away for a bit? I wondered if you had some friend you could go to. It would do Alex a power of good if you weren't here when he returned."

"I don't know. I hadn't really thought."

"Then don't you think it's time you did?"

By twelve o'clock, with almost diabolical efficiency, Cara had seen Sophie off at the station en route for Elizabeth and George.

19

"Of course, she wanted you gone." Elizabeth lay stretched out on one of her long garden chairs, a cup of tea balanced precariously on her stomach.

"Oh, I don't know. I think she was being quite kind really. After all, I was in a pretty good mess." Sophie had told Elizabeth everything, or more or less everything. She had not minimised the drinking, but she had found it difficult to say much about that intensely private relationship which, in any case, belonged to her and Alex alone, and one which Elizabeth, on her own admission, appeared never to have missed in life. In the circumstances, it seemed all the more creditable that she should be bothering about Sophie at all. The latter said as much.

"Just because I can't see anything of this sort happening to me, my dear, it doesn't mean I'm not very concerned about you and, to be quite frank, very interested in what you seem to have got yourself involved in. Since I came to stay with you I've felt that you were up against some pretty curious characters. I thought Cornish Cara was a particular force to be reckoned with and, as you know, that you might want a break from it all sometime, although I must say I didn't think you'd need it quite so soon."

"But it's Alex really. I mean, he's the problem, not Cara."

"Is he? But it was she who stopped you having your reconciliation."

Sophie shut her eyes. She knew Elizabeth was right on that point. She had not heard anything from Alex for a week now. She presumed Cara must have telephoned and told him what had happened. Why had she allowed herself to be bundled off like some parcel? Had she no will of her own? If she hadn't tried to alleviate the situation by alcohol, she might not have let Cara take such command. What sort of a weak fool was she to have sunk so low, to have become the slave to her own petty problems and a confused one at that? If one compared this tiny heaven and hell of a love affair with all the wider issues at stake in the world—wars, earthquakes, national disasters—one could hardly do other than despise oneself for the most appalling egotism. She had never been a woman to take much part in community life, had never, like Elizabeth, joined things, chaired meetings, organized fêtes; but she had known what was going on, helped where she felt she could, read a great deal in the interstices of, firstly, bringing up a delicate child and then, to a lesser degree, doing her duty by Hugh. How long was it now since she had read a book right through? She began to do things but somehow Alex, or what he required of her, put a stop to them. Even her re-awakened interest in painting had come to nought.

"And what, may I ask, are you two so busy not talking about? Any tea left in that pot?" George had come across the garden and sank down on the ·grass beside them. "Have you forgotten, Elizabeth, that we're due at the Wilkinsons' at six-thirty and it's over an hour's drive?"

"Oh, my God. Yes, I had. You go, George. Make my apologies. Say . . . say I've got a summer cold or something."

"Why don't we all go? They'd be charmed to see Sophie."

Elizabeth turned to her. "What about it? Would you like to?"

"I'd sooner not. But I'd hate it if you both didn't go. I'll be quite all right. Please. I want . . . to write some letters." She could see Elizabeth looking at her anxiously, knowing all too well the reason for it. She had not been actually left alone in the house since her arrival, but it was high time she was. She could not very well announce in front of George that she would not start drinking again because she guessed that Elizabeth, loyal friend that she was, would have told him only a fraction of the reason for her sudden visit. Over the top of George's head she said again, "I shall *truly* be all right."

She waved goodbye to them a little later, Elizabeth still having to be chivvied reluctantly into the car.

"I wish you'd come."

"No. I'd rather not. Supper will be all ready when you get back, I promise."

She went into the house. There was, she found, little to do in that direction except to lay the table and turn on the oven when the time came. Elizabeth might not be a particularly methodical housewife but she was the kind who always kept a full larder, who could invariably be relied on to produce a meal for any number of people with the minimum of effort or fuss. She had not been at all disconcerted at Sophie's sudden telephone call and subsequent arrival, and George had seemed to accept the situation equally calmly, as if it were perfectly natural for one of his beloved wife's friends to turn up for a self-invited visit at the ungodly hour of eleven thirty p.m. Not for the first time did Sophie envy and speculate on the security of a relationship which could embrace a third—at least temporarily—in such fashion.

She went up to the bedroom she was occupying and stood at the window looking down at the garden and the little meadow beyond, which her host and hostess had recently acquired. There were George's bees, there was the shed he had been creosoting earlier that day, there were Elizabeth's prize dahlias—all so splendid and commendable. What devilish motivation was it that propelled some people—from whatever walk of life they came—away from such domesticity? Boredom? Weakness of character? Inability to give and take? Too much money? Too little money? Failure to compromise? Or that devastating urgent physical need which, alone, seemed to be the only thing which gave someone like herself a sense of belonging? For over a year she had felt she belonged to another person as she had never done before. And she still felt that way. She certainly did not belong here, however welcome George and Elizabeth made her. Guiltily, she realised she had used them ungraciously and ungratefully. She would never be able to do for Elizabeth anything like that which she had invariably done for her. But then, somehow, she could not imagine Elizabeth needing anything done. She would never be cursed with what amounted to a sickness, a sickness one could become just as hooked on as alcohol or drugs. She had told Elizabeth that while she had been staying with them, the need for alcohol had decreased and this was, to a large extent, true. Their very company had helped to lessen the desire for the bottle. But it had not assuaged the desire for Alex. After the first forty-eight hours of vague relief, the longing for him had returned and intensified. She sat down and started to write him a letter.

She was surprised to hear the sound of a car coming up the drive, because she hadn't expected George and Elizabeth anything like so soon. She supposed Elizabeth had still been uneasy and insisted on returning early. She put down her pen and hurried downstairs to switch on the oven—so much for her promise to have everything ready. They did not immediately come into the house and she went to the front door to greet them. Alex was standing on the door-step.

20

On the way back to London she knew that she had behaved atrociously to George and Elizabeth. She had simply left them a note because Alex had been so insistent about getting on. "It's a three-hour drive, Dishy. I'd like to break the back of it before we stop and eat." He had paced about the garden while she threw her belongings into a suitcase, had remembered—just in time—to turn the oven down to 'Low', and worded some totally inadequate thanks and apologies which she placed on a large sheet of paper in the hall. She sensed that, above all things, Alex wanted to be away before what he referred to, naughtily, as "the squirearchy's" return.

Once on the road he drove, as usual, comparatively slowly and, for the most part, without speaking, simply dropping a hand on her knee every so often while they halted at traffic lights. He did not refer to her flight from Cornwall, or to Cara, or to why he had chosen this particular day and time to come and search her out. Occasionally, he hummed a little tuneless tune to himself and she knew he was happy, living in the present, and that, but for a few initial qualms about her recent hasty exit, she was happy also. Tomorrow she would write a long letter to Elizabeth.

London was quite autumnal during the September days which followed. Each morning when she woke, reassured by his presence beside her, she could see more leaves fluttering down from the sycamore trees as they made their haphazard, inconsequential journey into the gardens below. Before very long it would be Christmas, the first that she and Alex would have actually spent together and some-times, idly, before he woke, she began to make plans. Perhaps Jamie might come, just for a night or so. Her new way of life seemed somehow more established now, almost—if one could use the word—respectable, not the supposedly short-lived madness which she feared had originally given rise to so much speculation. It no longer mattered to her that she was Alex's mistress. He had wanted her back. She had wanted him back. It was as simple as that. There seemed, if anything, to be more love between them. Both had made this very plain in the days, and especially the nights, which had passed so swiftly and easily since their return to London. She felt much more sure of herself, and of him, even grateful to Cara for bringing about, albeit unconsciously perhaps, their temporary parting. The other woman had ceased to be a threat. Sophie knew that Alex often spoke to her on the telephone but not, by any means, in such a surreptitious way as before, and it was something she could now accept. On one occasion she had even spoke to her herself. If there was a hint of pique and disappointment in Cara's voice at finding Sophie so re-entrenched, the latter did her best to replace any feeling of satisfaction with that of sympathy. How could the poor woman, *any* woman, go on living with such an appalling handicap?

After a week or so, this kind of euphoria gave Sophie the confidence to bring up a question which she had never quite got around to doing before. They were still in bed, for some reason holding hands and staring at the spotty, discoloured ceiling.

"Alex, don't you think it's time some redecorating was

done in this house?"

He did not actually let go of her hand, but there was an almost imperceptible withdrawal of his fingers, as if her question had interfered with that precious, vital response between them.

"I don't think that's a very good idea, Dishy."

"Why not? If you're thinking about the expense, I thought it could be my Christmas present to you . . . to the home . . ." She had never understood his attitude to finance. There were times when he seemed on the verge of bankruptcy, others—especially after he had sold a picture or two—when his funds appeared limitless. She had no idea of his basic resources.

"My sweet, we may not be here at Christmas."

"Not here?" She turned her head quickly. He went on staring at the ceiling, his profile impassive. "What on earth do you mean?"

"Exactly what I say. I hadn't wanted to bother you just now. You seemed so particularly pleased with life. But I suppose you'll have to know soon. The Millets, the couple downstairs, are selling up. They're going into some old people's home in the country where they'll be looked after. I'm only a tenant on a three-yearly lease and the last three years will soon be up, I can't possibly afford to buy the place."

"Oh, *Alex!*" She had come to associate him so much with what she called his 'highline' home that it was impossible to think of him in any other surroundings. "Your studio . . ."

"I know."

"Is it quite definite?"

"Quite. Their daughter came up and appears to have arranged everything. Rather a managing female, I thought, but I suppose she knows what she's doing."

"But they can't turn you out just like that, can they? I mean, you're a sitting tenant."

"Sitting duck more like it. They're old, Dishy. I shan't make things difficult for them."

"When did you first know about it?"

He did not answer at once. "Oh, I can't remember. Not very long ago. Dishy dear, how about some breakfast?"

While she was in the kitchen the answer seemed perfectly clear, and when she returned with the tray she made her offer. Alex had not given the slightest hint in this direction. For all she knew, such an obvious solution had never occurred to him.

"I'm going to buy this house, Alex. Olivia's estate is almost bound to be wound up soon. I'm going to ring Bellinger this morning."

He did not say anything for some time and then he gave a wry grin. "And what does that make me, Dishy? A sort of kept man? Gigolo? Tenant? What rent might you be charging, madam?"

She acquired the whole house by mid-November. After a little amicable dissent, Alex gave in, almost with relief, keeping completely out of all negotiations and leaving every decision regarding improvements or decorating to her. "It's your home, Dishy. Go ahead. I'll like whatever you like."

She had been somewhat surprised that Olivia's estate had come well below the figure which Mr Bellinger had first given her to believe. There had, he explained, been unforeseen complications over back tax which had completely altered the picture and was why everything had taken so long to wind up. The prospect of having enough capital to help Hugh to buy a farm would appear to have been a chimera. She recalled his enthusiastic efforts in that direction and wondered what he would say now if he knew what had happened. Nevertheless, she was delighted at her present investment, sparing little expense in getting it just as she wanted it. Besides, it could all go to Jamie one day.

"Anyone might think," said Alex, at the beginning of December, on coming across her sitting on the floor surrounded by patterns of upholstery, "that you were *expecting*. I believe that sort of activity you're indulging in usually attacks a woman with child. But right now I'm hungry. Let's go out." The fact that she had invariably prepared some sort of meal never seemed to enter his head. Domesticity was beyond him. Actually, on this particular evening she was quite pleased to be taken out, for she had been working at the downstairs rooms all day. Whatever food there was could perfectly well wait until tomorrow.

Over the meal, when she was on her second glass of wine and feeling pleasantly relaxed, he said, àpropos of nothing very much, "I thought we might leave for Cornwall in a week or so's time."

"Cornwall?" She frowned. "You don't mean . . you're not thinking of going for *Christmas*, are you?"

"But of course. I always go to Cornwall for Christmas."

She put down her knife and fork and stared at him in mute disbelief.

"Don't look so theatrical, Dishy. You must know. I mean, surely you didn't think I'd leave Cara alone at Christmas, did you? And in any case, I want to see about getting the roof of Tremarthen repaired before the worst of the winter sets in."

"I'm afraid . . . I mean, I hadn't thought . . ." It was true. She had been so busy, so blissfully preoccupied on her new project that Cara had all but faded into obscurity, a silent burden which affected Alex alone and was really nothing to do with her.

"I must go, Dishy. She looks forward to it so."

The waiter removed her plate and asked if she would like a sweet, but she had ceased to feel hungry and shook her head. It was all so damnably vindicable. It was, on the face of it, very *nice* of Alex to feel so obligated. It was she who was mean-minded.

"I'm sorry. It's just . . . well, with the house beginning to look so good. Why don't we have Cara up to London . . . and perhaps Jamie for a night or two?" she added, lamely.

"Cara never comes to London. By all means have Jamie if you like, and I'll go down to be with her."

"You mean not spend Christmas together?"

"Sophie, my dear, we're together all the time. We needn't shed any tears over Christmas, need we? I know women set such store by these things, but personally it's never meant anything to me. If you really don't want to eat anything else, shall we go?"

21

"I don't quite see why you're alone?" Jamie sat sprawled in one of her newly-upholstered chairs. Someone called Arabella Hope-Finlayson sat in more or less an equally recumbent position in another.

"Alex has gone to spend Christmas with an old and handicapped friend. He always does."

"Uh-huh." Jamie, to her regret, was drinking whisky. Arabella had asked for vodka. Out of a ridiculous sense of sham propriety Sophie had elected to pour herself a dry sherry.

"Pity Alex's friend isn't up to coming to stay here, poor chap. Still, we're around to carve the turkey, pull the crackers, all that sort of thing, aren't we, Belle?" Arabella giggled. Sophie ignored Jamie's natural but mistaken assumption over the sex of Alex's friend. Presently, she watched her son get up and help himself casually to another drink. "How are you doing, Belle? What about you, Mummy?"

Arabella giggled again and held out her glass. Sophie

said, "Not for me at the moment." Jamie returned to his erstwhile spread-eagled position.

She couldn't quite put her finger on it but there was something about him which hadn't been so apparent when they had met in the summer: a kind of slackness, a nihilism, a couldn't-care-less attitude. She supposed it had taken hold after he had flunked his A-levels, about which she had been both surprised and distressed. She knew that he had just re-taken one of them, but was horrified to hear what he now proposed to do. It appeared that, for a year at least, he intended to live in Australia and become a Jackaroo. She supposed that the work could, conceivably, be the making of him, but it saddened her to think that any chance of an academic or even artistic career seemed to have been completely ruled out.

He spoke defensively about his plans, as if he were basically against her, as if she had been the primary reason for his failure in other directions.

"Dad thinks it a good idea. In fact, he suggested it."

"Did he? When do you leave?"

"First of Feb. Belle and I are going on a ski-ing holiday to Verbier first." Arabella giggled once more. Sophie began to wonder if the girl would or could do anything else as a contribution to a visit which had already got off to an extremely bad start.

She wanted to ask Jamie many things: how, for instance, was he managing for money? what sort of allowance was Hugh giving him? how were things at home? But she felt unable to bring up any of these subjects in front of his girl-friend. She had not bargained on having to entertain her also. Jamie had merely accepted Sophie's invitation to come for Christmas with, "As long as you don't mind two of us." She had taken an instant dislike to the young woman now two-thirds of the way through her second drink, to those pale curtains of hair which all but obscured the pale, pert little face and the small, podgy figure girded into its tight sweater and dirty jeans—why had anyone ever invented such an unattractive garment?—and the scruffy shoes which had been kicked off, as a concession, or so Sophie hoped, to the new chair-covers on which her young body was now curling up like a cat.

It was, perhaps, no mere accident that Sophie had put Arabella in the little blue room along the corridor from where she herself would be sleeping, and Jamie in one of the furthermost bedrooms in that other part of the house which had only recently been acquired. She was well aware that such tactics would not prevent the inevitable, that she was presumably meant to turn a blind eye to whatever took place in the night. Besides, what sort of God-awful hypocrite was she? Did she have one set of morality for her son, another for herself? What right had she to act the censor in the circumstances in which they both knew her to be living? She was the last person who could come the heavy mother now. She wondered what Jamie really thought about her. Did he and Arabella speculate and giggle in private over her *modus vivendi*? Or weren't they interested? Was her son's present unsatisfactory behaviour her fault? Was she really the cause of his poor examination results? Had the fact that his mother had "gone off the rails" affected him far more than she cared to suppose or admit? The present-day young were said to be tolerant, but just how tolerant were they really, deep down? When she had been eighteen she would have been horrified at the thought of Olivia indulging in some sexual spree. But then one couldn't possibly imagine Olivia, with her twin sets and pearls, ever having so much as parted her legs. Yet she must have done, once, or she herself wouldn't be here now. And when she came to think about it, her mother had sometimes behaved quite coyly when old Bellinger had come to dinner.

The conversation flagged and she could think of little to revive it. She was odd man—or woman—out in this ill-assorted trio. There seemed no common ground on which to meet, even though Jamie was her son. Had the girl not been there, she felt she might have got through to him, but Arabella's presence seemed to inhibit even the most superficial small talk. Sophie did, at last, get around to enquiring what Hugh would be doing for Christmas.

"Oh, he's got it all tricked out. Sunningdale's pretty social, you know. He gets asked out a lot." Was there an exchange of glances between the two young people? She couldn't be sure. They seemed to have some silent, secret inexplicable means of communication from which she was totally excluded. In desperation she stood up.

"I think it's time I saw about dinner."

"Oh, don't worry about us tonight, Mummy. I forgot to say. There's a film on at Leicester Square that we want to see. We'll get something to eat later. You take it easy. If you'll just let me have a key, we won't wake you up."

She hoped her voice sounded normal. "Of course, I'll go and fetch it." In the end she threw it over the banisters and wished them good-night from there. Then she went back into her bedroom and lay down. She was not sure how she was going to get through the next few days. It was all turning out to be so much worse than she had feared. She wanted to ring Alex and ask him to come back. How *could* he have deserted her now. She should never have allowed him to. She should have forgotten about Jamie and gone to Cornwall and she and Cara and Alex could all have spent Christmas together. Anything would have been preferable to what was happening. She would like to have rung Elizabeth, but although the latter's good nature seemed limitless, there was also a limit to what she felt she had any right to expect. And anyway, unless she wanted to lose Jamie completely, she would have to go through Christmas with him and his wretched girl-friend somehow. Besides, ringing Elizabeth for moral support would mean more explanations. She hadn't been quite truthful when Elizabeth had asked her about her plans a few weeks earlier. "Alex may spend a few days in Cornwall at the beginning of Christmas week . . ." Not even to her best friend would she admit that he would be away on Christmas Day.

If only there was someone of her own generation whom she could ring up and ask round. But all the people she knew in London were Alex's friends and, anyway, older. She had allowed herself to live through him. To let Vincent or any of them know that, three days before Christmas, she was alone, would mean explaining a situation which even the most unconventional and uncritical would find highly questionable. They would not know just how extraordinary and complicated Alex was. One had to live with him to appreciate that. In any case, they would mostly all be fixed up or away by now. Vincent seemed to be often in the country. There were really only two things one could do about her present liaison: take it or leave it. And she wasn't, she knew now, strong enough to leave it. She was inescapably trapped. She was prepared to sacrifice self-respect, self-control, independence, anything, in fact, for the sake of . . . She shut her eyes. Was it for love or something which often passed as such, something which, this very night, she was doing her best to deny her son.

22

Alex returned after tea on Boxing Day, an hour or so after Jamie and Arabella had left for Sunningdale in order to attend—as her son ungraciously put it—"some nosh-up of Dad's". Shedding scarf, coat and a curious yellow knitted hat, which he informed her was one of Cara's Christmas presents to him, he settled himself untidily into the new drawing-room. He seemed in extremely good spirits, just as he had been when he telephoned her on Christmas Day.

"On the dot, Dishy. I promised I'd be back by six, didn't I? How did your maternal act go?"

Had he simply forgotten how she had once reacted to a similar remark? She tried to keep reproach from her voice. "Not particularly well. I didn't like the girl. They went out quite a lot. The rest of the time I think they were rather bored."

"Really? Still, you've done your duty and I've done mine. Or half of it."

"Half?"

"My love, don't look like some startled filly. You must try

to curb your facial expressions. I'm not leaving you again
for a bit. But on the way home I thought it was high time I
saw Martina again. Do you realise that I haven't been over
to France since I've known you?"

"But I thought you said she didn't want you to go. I
mean, that your visits upset her?"

"Did I? Well, that's true in a sense. But if I don't go once in
a way, I don't really know what's going on, do I? You must
remember that I do finance the set-up. And her companion
is an extremely taciturn woman. Sometimes I think she has
too much control. She's never liked me and hasn't bothered
to hide the fact. I haven't been altogether happy about one
or two of Martina's brief communiqués lately."

She bent down to pick up Alex's scarf lying like some
menacing, green snake between them, hoping that this
would prevent him from noticing the colour which had
suddenly come to her face. What communiqués? When had
he had them? Why couldn't he have told her? Would it
always be like this? Would he live the rest of his life, as she
saw it, in chains? Fettered by two women for whom, try as
she might, she could feel no honest sympathy.

He appeared to ignore her silence. "So I thought that,
perhaps, in the spring, we might go to Paris. April in Paris.
That would be fun, wouldn't it, Dishy. You'd love it. And
then I'll leave you only for a few days and go down to the
Dordogne and find out what's going on."

"I see." She had recovered her composure a little. He had
given the pill an almost diabolical coating of sugar. Whatever else there was to be said against living with Alex, it was
never dull. Just when one began to flag or to feel resentful,
he seemed to inject excitement into life like some powerful
drug. He knew just when to administer the needle, just
when to withhold. He could even, on occasion, stir up
desire and then keep her waiting and wanting as, for
instance, tonight. He knew how much she had missed him,
how much, despite her underlying anger and indignation at
being left over Christmas, she longed to be made love to
again and, what was more, how furious she was with
herself for this being so. He sat in the armchair opposite her,
very much alive for all his long journey, amused, apprais-

ing—she was wearing a new dress—and hugely self-confident. Then he held out his arms. "Dishy, my sweet. Come here. I still find you just as sexually inviting as when I first saw you. Especially when your nurture/nature battle is going on inside. That's something of a record, I think."

In the weeks that followed, she reflected several times on that statement, feeling it to be as true a one as he had probably ever made to her. That part of their lives still seemed as mutually pleasurable as it had been in the beginning. In this sphere she had, as it were, surprised herself. She supposed, if she tried to analyse it at all, the fact that he had broken through what amounted to a hitherto cast-iron conventionality and found what he had rightly suspected underneath, still intrigued him. "It's like making love to a pro," he had said on one occasion and, far from feeling insulted, she had taken it as a compliment. She began looking forward to Paris enormously.

Alex happened to be out when the call came through from France one day towards the end of March. As she hung on, listening to the cacophony of foreign voices, she was distressed that he was not there to receive news which, she felt certain, could not be other than urgent and important. Presently, a woman speaking good, though heavily accented, English came on the end of the line asking for him.

"I'm sorry. Mr Dolan is out."

"Who am I speaking to?"

She hesitated. "My name is Mrs Brent."

"I see. I have some sad news, I'm afraid. Would you please tell him that Mrs Dolan died this morning. Could he come at once, please."

"Yes. I'm sorry. Of course."

She put down the receiver. How could she reach him? He had told her that one of his prospective customers—as he called his sitters—had asked him to lunch at some club. She had no idea which one. There was nothing to do but sit and wait. Three, four and five o'clock came and still there was no sign of him. A different, sickening unease drove away the even baser emotion which had begun to take hold when she had first heard the news: now that Martina was dead . . . She began pacing about the flat. Where *was* Alex? Had she been living in a fool's paradise, relying too much on those words he had spoken when he came back after Christmas? Why hadn't she paid more attention to his plans for today? Was he, in fact, lunching with a customer at all? When she at last heard the sound of his key in the lock, she began running to the door and then checked herself. She must not be precipitate. She was not sure exactly how he would take what she had to tell him.

He came in jauntily, carrying a hat-box. "Open up, Dishy. I knew you had to have it as soon as I saw it in the window."

"Alex, I . . ."

"Open *up*, Darling. It's a present. To wear in Paris."

The hat-box came between them, incongruous, un-wieldly and hugely white. She found herself clutching it. She hitched it to one side of her and saw his face fall. "Alex I . . . please listen. I've something important to say . . ." At last she had his attention.

He seemed stunned at the news. He sat down suddenly on one of the hall chairs, staring at her in disbelief. "Oh my God," he said, at length. "I should have gone before. I should have gone. I told you, didn't I?" There was an angry tone in his voice now. "You wouldn't believe me. I know I should have gone over. Not waited till April. But I thought you'd enjoy Paris more then."

She stood there silently, alternately rejecting and accepting blame. The hat box felt heavy in her arms, like a proof of guilt.

23

After confusion and uncertainty connected with a temporarily mislaid passport and several long and not entirely satisfactory telephone calls to airlines, his bank and the continent, Alex departed early next morning. At midday, after she had brought order to the chaos which, in moments of stress, he seemed to generate like ectoplasm, she sat down and rang Elizabeth to ask her if she would like another holiday in London. She could sense the other's hesitancy almost before she spoke, and feared that it was because she had already demanded too much of a hitherto unstinted friendship. Neither was it any relief when she heard the real reason for Elizabeth's unwillingness to leave home.

"I'd love to, Sophie. But it's George. He's not been well since Christmas. Most unlike him. The doctor can't seem to find anything specific. I'm trying to get him away somewhere really warm if I can, but I'm having an awful job persuading him. How are things with you?"

Sophie told her, but briefly. In view of what she had just

heard, it hardly seemed the time to go into the personal, egoistical complications of being what she was well aware the media referred to nowadays as a "live-in" girl-friend. Faced with the prospect of her own company for an unspecified time, she decided to do the thing which she now knew from bitter experience to be impossible when Alex was around: paint. He couldn't, surely, object to her using his studio? Even though her own equipment was still languishing in Cornwall, she could buy some more. I will be disciplined, she kept telling herself. Office hours. With a kind of despairing desperation, she embarked on a view of rooftop London.

At the end of a week *Highline*, as she had come to think of her effort, surprised her. She felt that it was good, that it had something, but she couldn't be sure. She was putting the finishing touches to it one morning when the door-bell rang. Unexpected callers were not very frequent and she went downstairs wondering who it could be. Vincent Matheson stood on the doorstep. It was some time since he had come to sit for Alex and for a moment, in his cap and duffle-coat, she could hardly place him.

"Oh Vincent, how nice. Do come in."

He hesitated. "I don't want to disturb Alex."

"You won't be disturbing Alex. He's in France." She ushered him into the hall, and on into the new drawing-room.

"How nice this is. I didn't know Alex had this part of the house now."

"The previous owners wanted to get out." She saw no point in explaining that it belonged to her.

"You've made this charming."

"Thank you." She offered and he accepted a sherry.

"I called because I happened to be passing. I walk a lot these days. Retirement doesn't suit me, really. And also . . ." he hesitated again, and an almost sheepish grin came over his face. "Well, as a matter of fact, I did have another reason. I wanted to ask Alex about taking up painting. I suppose I'm too old, but I've always been interested. I thought he might know of the best places for the likes of me."

"What a splendid idea. I'm sure he'd be only too delighted to help." Would he really, she wondered? Alex had so little time for amateurs.

Vincent sat on, spare and neat and smiling, a little uncertain what and what not to ask. Gently, she helped him. "Alex has had to go to France because his wife has just died."

"I'm sorry. I never knew . . . about a wife, I mean."

"They've lived apart for a long time."

"I see." He allowed her to refill his glass. "My own wife died many years ago now." He seemed to be suddenly back in the past.

It was her turn to commiserate. She felt they had somehow got on to difficult territory. Presently, she asked him if he would like to see the rest of the house and he accepted with alacrity. When they reached the studio and he came face to face with *Highline*, he stopped and gave a little gasp. Then he turned to her, puzzled. "Alex's . . ?"

"No, mine, as a matter of fact."

His astonishment and appreciation were so genuine that she became violently elated. She would go on painting. She *must* go on. She could hardly believe his next words.

"Is it for sale?"

Taken aback, she floundered. She had planned, vaguely, if Alex had been approving, to make a present of it to him. But she knew he could so easily be critical, in which case . . . "I haven't really thought. It's the first I've done for ages . . ."

"Will you let me know, when you've decided? I have the very place for it in my home."

They went back downstairs. He lingered in the hall, as if he were about to say something and then thought better of it. After he had gone she sat for a long time, thinking. Vincent Matheson was lonely. He made it plain how much he liked her, but that he also knew she belonged to Alex. The Vincent Mathesons of this world were as different from the Alex Dolans as rock and quicksand. With Vincent one would be protected, cherished, worshipped, almost. There would be no more uncertainty, hurt, being kept in the dark, sudden partings, no other women to worry about. Vincent Matheson could and would provide every single thing— except one.

24

She was planting up window boxes outside the first-floor rooms when Alex returned, without warning, one Sunday just after lunch. She waited while he paid off the taxi and then called out a greeting to him as he came up the steps. He gave a quick nod but did not smile. When she opened the front door he looked as if he had aged about ten years.

In the hall, he neither kissed her nor said anything other than, "Those damned flights. I should have been back yesterday."

"Have you eaten?"

"No, but I'm not hungry. I think I'll go to bed."

He lumbered upstairs carrying his suitcase. She heard him go into the bedroom and close the door. Uncertainly, she went on with her miniature gardening efforts.

When it got to seven o'clock and he still had not re-appeared, she decided he had been left alone long enough. However tired, whatever ordeal he appeared to have been through, there seemed no excuse for this kind of home-coming. She went upstairs, threw open the door and found him lying with his hands clasped behind his head, staring at the opposite wall.

"Alex."

"Yes." He did not turn to look at her.

"What's the matter? Aren't you coming down to eat tonight?"

"Why d'you keep harping on food? I've told you. I'm not hungry."

"Well, surely, a drink or something. Was it . . . was it that bad?"

"Need we go into it? She's dead. I've done what was necessary."

She wanted to know, but refrained from asking, why "what was necessary" had taken over three weeks. Where had he stayed? Surely not all the time with Martina's companion, a woman he did not like. He had told her so little over the telephone. For the past week his calls had ceased altogether and more than once she had been on the point of ringing him. Had his wife's death really affected him so drastically? He couldn't be grieving, surely. After all, there appeared to have been no love lost between them for years. Could he still be blaming her, Sophie, for the fact that he hadn't been over to see Martina for so long? Was he, in some extraordinary way, switching the blame from Cara to herself, holding her responsible in his incomprehensible mind for something which happened before she ever knew him? She had long been aware that when things went wrong he had to have a whipping-boy—or woman.

The room, as always after one of his sudden re-appearances, was in disarray, strewn with accoutrements: odd socks, several dirty shirts and a heap of loose documents, spilling across the floor like some paper-chase, from his half-empty suitcase. She went across to deal with the offending mess.

"Leave it." With extraordinary swiftness for one so seemingly exhausted, he was out of bed, pulling her away, roughly. "I'll see to everything. I want to sort through my papers. There wasn't time before leaving."

Without another word, she turned and left him. For the first time since they had been living together, she went into another room for the night.

It had never once occurred to her that Alex might have done anything else while he was away. When, a few days later, she was giving Mrs Tuffnell the rest of his dirty washing and, after doing so, noticed a scrap of paper lying on the floor which must have fallen from the crumpled armful, she picked it up casually to place in the waste-paper basket. Only when the word Lausanne caught her eye, did she pause and look at it again. It was a torn single rail ticket dated ten days previously. But he had been nowhere near Switzerland, at least not that she knew of—until now.

Constraint, estrangement came between them, almost tangible, she felt, like double glazing. She could *see* Alex, she was aware of his every movement, but he was on the other side of an impenetrable window, carrying on some private life in which he did not want her to share. Hurt and nonplussed, she retreated into one of her own. *Highline*, the picture which she had so looked forward to showing him, remained hidden in a cupboard. Often he went out, she knew not where. Left alone of an evening, she began doing something from which she had managed to refrain since Cornwall. The level in successive gin bottles sank rapidly. Finding that this way sleep, of a kind, came more quickly, she deluded herself that it was preferable to resorting to sleeping pills. Yet she was apt to wake suddenly at two, three of four o'clock and find her night's rest over.

On one such early morning she woke with a start to find Alex sitting on the end of her bed. In the greyish light he looked ill and dejected. Almost nervously, he held out a hand.

"Dishy?"

She accepted his overture, placing one of her hands in his, but remained silent.

"I've given you a bad time. I'm sorry."

"Thank you."

"I suppose you've been wondering . . . you must have . . . why I took so long . . . coming back."

"Yes."

"I went to Lausanne, as a matter of fact."

"I know."

"You *know*? Oh God, spying on me, I take it, looking for clues? You've every right, I suppose . . ."

"No. It was quite accidental. A torn rail ticket fell out of your washing."

He sighed. "I have several friends near there. I was frightened to come back."

"*Frightened*? What of?"

"You."

"*Me*?" She wondered whether one or the other of them was suffering from delusions.

"You must *see*, Dishy. I'm what they call a free man, now. No longer a semi-detached one. I thought sooner or later you'd be bound to get divorced and put the pressure on. You'd want to regularize our relationship. I believe that's the term people use. After all, you do have a very strong conventional streak in you, like the rest of your sex, I'm afraid."

She was silent again. How could the thought not have crossed her mind? She knew, and presumably Alex knew, that however much women protested to the contrary, most of them were lying when they said they would prefer to remain unmarried to the man they were living with. On the other hand, she hoped she would never have resorted to the pressure to which he referred.

"I shan't marry, Dishy. You might as well know at once. There's Cara to consider. It would more or less finish her now. She's getting older. I'm all she has left."

"Yes. I understand."

"Please go on doing so." He gathered her in his arms. "You will, won't you, Dishy?"

They were back, for a few weeks, where they were. Alex, in fact, appeared to be in better form than ever. He was asked to undertake several new commissions and seemed altogether more loving, more considerate and kinder in every way. Just why Sophie still felt so depressed she found hard to tell. With Jamie writing happily and enthusiastically from Australia, her old life well in the past, several amusing joint invitations and a particularly pleasant—almost hilarious—evening with Vincent Matheson and his younger brother, she was at a loss to account for an unaccustomed lassitude, a feeling—mostly in the early mornings—of blankness, of the day before her stretching ahead bleakly, heavy and without purpose, something to be got through by someone who was simply treading water in some unknown, stagnant pool. The smallest things began to upset her: a cup that was broken, a stocking that suddenly laddered. All added up to some joint personal vendetta against her. Even the gathering-up of the morning's post was an added affront, confirming her own uselessness and unimportance in the preponderance of letters for Alex compared to those for herself.

It was so long since she had read Hugh's handwriting that when, one morning, she found an envelope for herself marked "Personal", she was momentarily almost pleased. Then, realising the identity of the sender, she retreated into the room she had turned into a small study for herself and slit the envelope open apprehensively. Its contents were typically Hugh: brief and to the point.

Dear Sophie,

I thought I should warn you that you will shortly be hearing from my solicitors, as I have asked them to petition for a divorce. This may come as a surprise, as at one time you will remember that I did not want one. I have, however, had the great good fortune to find someone I wish to marry—and vice versa—at the earliest possible date, and I therefore do not want to wait until the statutory two years of living apart is up next January, when we might have divorced by mutual consent. I shall be citing Alex Dolan as co-respondent . . .

The last two lines of the letter began to dance up and down, as the hand which was holding it began to shake, uncontrollably.

25

Mr Gregory, the solicitor with whom Sophie found herself closeted in the firm of Bates, Gregory and Hardcastle, seemed about as impersonal as the letter from Hugh which she had just passed him to read. Everything about him appeared grey and remote and somehow disapproving, as if all he really wanted to do was to disassociate himself from her and her problems right at the start. He had not smiled when she entered his dun-coloured office in the Strand. He had merely stood up, reluctantly she felt, and held out a small, limp hand with, "Good-afternoon, Mrs Brent. What can I do for you?" And she had frowned because she had already, in her letter, told the firm of Bates, Gregory and Hardcastle what they could do for her, and she had no means of knowing that this was Mr Gregory senior's habitual method of greeting new clients. Even Mr Bellinger would have been decidedly more comforting than this dreary, weary and seemingly uninterested little man. But then, Mr Bellinger was retiring and, anyway, he was in Cheshire and had never really "done" divorces.

So she had found Bates, Gregory and Hardcastle in the Yellow Pages of the London Telephone Directory; but now that she was within their premises she wished that she had taken more trouble to get some personal recommendation to a solicitor, however much she wanted to keep her affairs private. She felt that she and Mr Gregory had somehow got off to a bad start. He had made her nervous and she had dropped her gloves, so she had quickly given him Hugh's letter to cover her embarrassment.

Mr Gregory took an unconscionable time studying it. It might have been a six-page epistle rather than something written on only one side of a sheet of writing-paper, and a small sheet at that. The silence in the room became as oppressive as the heat. She felt herself breaking out into a sweat. Presently, Mr Gregory looked up, whipped off his half-moon spectacles with surprising alacrity, placed his elbows on his desk and rested his small pointed chin on his clasped finger-tips. Except for his little grey eyes now directed straight towards her, he might have been in an attitude of prayer.

"And how do you feel about your husband's letter, Mrs Brent?"

"I . . . well, I suppose we'd better have a divorce. I mean, that's what I've come about."

"And this Mr Dolan? What does he feel? Does he intend to marry you?"

"No." She did not say that after reading Hugh's letter Alex had become violently angry and had now taken himself off to Cornwall.

"Why doesn't Mr Dolan wish to marry you? Is he married?"

"No." She was aware she was becoming monosyllabic.

Mr Gregory frowned and looked down at the letter again.

"Other than your desire to be with Mr Dolan, Mrs Brent, were there any other reasons which made you finally leave your husband? I mean, was the marriage happy before Mr Dolan came on the scene?"

"No." That's three 'Nos' in a row, she thought. Miserably, she looked past Mr Gregory and out of the window.

She could see a different 'Highline' from where she was
sitting, and wondered if she would ever get around to
showing Alex the first. She found it difficult to concentrate
on what this unprepossessing little man was saying to her.
She somehow felt that had this same interview taken place
when she had first left Hugh, it would have affected her
quite differently. She wouldn't have minded. She would
have made light of it. Something to laugh about afterwards—with Alex. But Alex wasn't there to laugh with.
Alex was down in Cornwall seeking refuge with one
woman from another whose problems had become too
much for him. She was vaguely aware that Mr Gregory was
looking at her quizzically. "I was saying . . ." he began,
and she supposed she had not been paying attention.

"You wouldn't like to tell me why your marriage wasn't
happy, would you, Mrs Brent?" Her inquisitor's voice was
suddenly more gentle. "I mean, perhaps there were exten-
uating circumstances connected with your departure,
which might affect any financial settlement?"

"Settlement?"

"Well, that's what divorce is all about, isn't it?"

She was hot and bothered and angry now. Was that all he
was thinking about? The money? She had come to him
because Hugh wanted a divorce, had already consulted
solicitors, and she felt, therefore, that she had to do likewise. She neither expected, needed, nor wanted any
alimony. She supposed that she was a disappointing client
for this man before her. She wished he would open a
window.

"I have private means, Mr Gregory. As it is I who am
being petitioned, for all I know the boot may be on the other
foot . . ." Her voice rose, agitatedly. She felt she would like
a drink.

"What about children?"

"I . . . we have one son, of eighteen. He's out in
Australia."

"I see." Mr Gregory seemed to be looking more and more
unhappy, as if he were being confronted by something he
didn't really see at all.

"I mean, it's quite straightforward, isn't it? I'm the so-called "guilty party". I'm not defending the case. My husband didn't want a divorce before and now he does . . ." An imaginary picture of Hugh's intended floated vaguely into her mind, like a blurred negative super-imposing itself on another. She wondered idly how the sex side of such a union would work. The vision faded and she became aware of Mr Gregory again, looking definitely uneasy. She began to speak quickly. It was difficult to get things across. "I left my husband because . . . he couldn't . . . give me . . ." Mr Gregory's face receded and then came forward again, like a Cheshire cat. There was a curious blackness revolving round it.

A young woman was bending over her when she came round, a kind-looking, moon-faced young woman who held a glass of water in one hand and was looking at her anxiously. Behind her, Mr Gregory hovered uncertainly. Fainting in solicitor's offices was not perhaps unheard of, but probably rare.

"You gave us a scare, Mrs Brent. How are you feeling?"

"I shall be quite all right." She made a move to get up and the large, white-faced young woman laid an arm on her shoulder. "Wait a little longer."

A cooler air seemed to have penetrated the room. She took a sip of water. Thank God someone had opened a window.

"There will be somebody at home, I take it, when you return? Perhaps I should telephone . . ?"

"No. Yes. I mean, I'm perfectly capable . . . If you could just get me a taxi."

"You're *sure* Mrs Brent? I don't feel you should be alone. You didn't look well when you first came in. You will call your doctor, won't you?"

"Yes, yes of course." She did not have a London doctor, had been fortunate in not wanting one since she had been living there, but anything to get away from Mr Gregory. She got up awkwardly and sat in one of his more comfort-able chairs while his secretary rang for a taxi.

"Perhaps you would like to let me know how you feel about everything in a few days, Mrs Brent, and tell me if you have any further, or maybe different, thoughts about a divorce."

Even in her enfeebled state, she was able to assure him that she simply wanted to get it over with.

26

Although Sophie knew that Mr Gregory's advice about seeing a doctor was sound and perfectly reasonable, she could think up various excuses for putting off taking it. The fact that she had been fortunate enough not to need a general practitioner since living in London was one of them, although she knew it was not really justifiable, for she had only to get in touch with Vincent Matheson and she would immediately be given the best advice possible. But the real reason she fought shy of the medical world was that she was aware of what was wrong and felt that no doctor, pill or potion was going to put it right. Moreover, she would be asked questions about herself and her problems. It had been bad enough with Mr Gregory but a doctor would probe much deeper. If she did not tell the truth perhaps he would attribute her malaise to the change of life. Even if this were a contributory factor, she did not want her *modus vivendi* of the past two years put down to some hormone imbalance. The thought horrified her.

Surely, if she were calm, patient and sensible, Alex

would return and they would "pick up" again, as they had done before. But looked at logically in the light of past events, she knew that such periods of harmony were short-lived. Alex seemed to need and almost deliberately manu-facture stress. It was like living on the end of a see-saw. Yet if she asked herself whether the 'highs' were worth the 'lows', regrettably, however much she may have wished it otherwise, the answer came back "Yes", even though the lows were now getting longer and more frequent. She couldn't live without Alex. He had become a necessary part of her, like elixir. Whenever he went away or went into one of his unpredictable moods, she suffered from withdrawal symptoms. She knew it was childish, even ridiculous, but she wished he would sometimes leave Hob with her, the little wooden mascot who had done so much to bring them together all those years ago in the Harley Street waiting-room. Hob would have helped in this empty London home which, so unaccountably, was now her own, a place where she had begun to feel captive emotionally, physically, prac-tically and economically. She could not suddenly walk out on it, as Alex appeared to do with such ease. She had bought it, expecting them both to go on living there. It had been a convenient arrangement which, at the time, had seemed to suit them both. And even now, she knew Alex would not willingly want to give up all that it meant to him. Unless she pulled out and sold it over his head—which she had no intention of doing—he would presumably continue to come and go as he pleased. However humiliating, she supposed she would allow him so to do. In other words, she was prepared to accept him at any price.

With an effort, she attempted to start painting again. But it had been one thing to produce *Highline* when Alex had gone away for a perfectly valid reason, or, at least, what initially appeared to be one. But now, it was another matter. The days dragged on, merging into equally interminable nights. August came to London, stifling and summer-weary. The streets were dusty, débris-strewn and full of foreign tourists; the house, although affording refuge of a kind, became more and more like a white elephant, large, unused and heavy with memories.

Still Alex did not come back. She posted on his mail and took to spending many hours simply lying on her bed. She had several conversations on the telephone with Elizabeth and although the latter did not put her fears into so many words, she gathered George's condition was due to the dread disease she had first suspected and that, after a temporary recovery, he was now very much worse. She did not attempt to get in touch with anyone else and no one got in touch with her. In any case, most people were away and she was in many ways relieved that there were no others to witness her in her present state. She sent Mrs Tuffnell on holiday and simply existed. Vincent Matheson wrote from the Alpes Maritimes, where he had rented a villa, imploring them both to come and stay with him. She merely forwarded the letter to Alex with no covering note. Sometimes, lying down of an evening with a drink beside her, the curtains partially drawn, she felt she could easily pass, unnoticed, into permanent oblivion, while London hummed and thrummed around her. Initially, this sensation caused a certain panic; after several gins, a hopeless resignation.

On one such evening, at about nine o'clock, the telephone rang. Unaware that her voice was slurred, she picked up the receiver, hoping—though against hope—it might be Alex. On hearing foreign operators, she wondered vaguely whether he had somehow gone abroad again.

"Sophie?"

"Yesh."

"Vincent here." There was a pause. "Are you all right?"

She did not answer at once, unable to appreciate who was calling. Her mind seemed to be revolving, taking an eternity to come to some conclusion.

"Oh, *Vinshent!*"

There was another pause, a longer one. She wondered whether he had rung off and she should put the receiver down.

"Sophie." The word was peremptory now. "Sophie. Are you alone?"

"Yesh. All alone Vinshent."

"Did you get my letter? Asking you and Alex to come

down here?"

Again she was a long time replying. The invitation was hazy in her mind. It could have been this year, last year, sometime . . . "I think so, Vinshent. I sent it . . . to Alex."

"Where is Alex?"

"Alex ish with Cara."

"Cara?"

"Yesh. In Cornwall." The pause was even longer now. She held on to the receiver, hopefully. It was nice of Vincent to ring . . . so long since she had spoken to anyone.

"Sophie." There was no kindness in his voice now. The next question was harsh, to the point, a doctor asking a devious patient for a specific reply. "How many drinks have you had?"

"Oh, Vinshent, I really don't know . . ."

"No more tonight, you understand. You heard me, Sophie? No more." There was a click and she was disconnected: disconnected from Vincent, from the world around her. Its noise receded and she fell asleep.

The trouble about drinking herself into insensibility each night meant that not only was the awakening abrupt and early, but also utterly bleak and chastening. The following morning she could remember little of the previous evening's conversation. Vincent Matheson had, she thought, telephoned, and been censorious. When he appeared at the front door early that evening, she was not only perplexed to see him in the flesh but also at the continuance of his terse, decisive manner which she had hitherto never come across. It was a very different Vincent who followed her into the drawing-room he had lately so admired. He looked at her dispassionately, almost clinically it seemed, from the other side of the fireplace. She did not know this Vincent and she felt both mortified and afraid.

"How long have you been alone?"

"I don't know. Five or six weeks perhaps."

"Who is this Cara?"

"An old friend." She corrected herself. "An old *girl*-friend." She answered cautiously, as sparing of words as the questions themselves.

"And you have been prepared to accept this?"

"Yes, but . . ."

"But what?"

"It's not quite what you think. She's . . . handicapped. Devoted, but handicapped."

He nodded, almost as if he had heard it all before. "Convenient."

"How do you mean?"

"Obligation in one direction can absolve someone from obligation in another."

She was silent.

"What do you intend to do?"

"Do? Nothing."

"You know that it . . . he will destroy you?"

"That's my business."

"So you'll go on. Why don't you just move out?"

"It's not that easy, Vincent. Last winter I bought this house. It's mine."

"My God." For a moment he covered his face in his hands. Presently he said, "Look, I intend to return to France tomorrow. I have other guests and several commitments. Will you come with me?"

It was very still in the room. She had not bothered to open up the windows or draw the curtains that morning. In the half-light she could see him, incredibly neat, despite his casual travelling clothes, a blue necktie at his throat, a pale linen jacket, looking utterly respectable, deeply concerned, willing her to accept his offer.

"I can't, Vincent. But thank you. Thank you so very much."

She was quite unprepared for his next statement, one which he must have already considered, knowing what her answer would be. "Then you must go to St Margaretta's."

"Where?"

"St Margaretta's. A hostel, nursing-home, call it what you will. For people like you."

The last four words hurt more than perhaps any which Alex had ever said to her. She bent her head. Realising that he had gone too far, he came across and knelt beside her and took her hand. "Sophie, my dear. You must see. You

must know. I care . . . I care too much to let you go the way
you're going. Someone's got to look after you. Please. I can
make all the arrangements."

27

St Margaretta's was not at all what she had imagined. For one thing it was not run by nuns, it was twenty miles out of London, there was very little surveillance and few rules. A woman doctor of about her own age came and talked to her in the garden most afternoons, but not about personal problems. Their conversation might have been that embarked upon at any social gathering. They touched on every conceivable general topic: politics, prices, religion, books, art. In order not to appear too ignorant, Sophie was forced to read the papers properly each morning, listen to the radio, look at television in the evenings. This, if nothing else, brought home to her how appallingly self-absorbed she had allowed herself to become. As she began to look outwards, so did the desire to retreat with a drink decrease. It was not until she had been at the Home a week that Dr Cheriton brought up the question of why she was where she was. Haltingly, Sophie told her. It was, of course, impossible to condense so much into a short space of time but she gave what she hoped was an honest account of the salient facts. She was listened to calmly and attentively, without that impassiveness which she had always understood any therapist adopted. Dr Cheriton was responsive, occasionally interrupting to comment or ask her to elucidate on some point.

"I make no hard and fast rules," she said, at length, "about giving advice. In any case, most people after they've been here a little while and start feeling better, simply begin to work things out for themselves. You're intelligent enough to do that, I'm sure. It seems that somewhere, perhaps a long time ago, you just missed the way. You know, really, don't you, that your present way of life is no good. That it can't go on."

"Yes."

"And that you mustn't expect, that it wouldn't be fair, to transfer yourself and your problems on to someone else's shoulders."

"Yes."

"I can see that the acquisition of this particular house you're living in may present problems. But they're not insurmountable. Have you thought of disposing of it and going to live somewhere where you've never been before? Make a fresh start?"

"Not . . . exactly."

"You know, until one has learnt to live alone, one usually makes a hash of living with someone else. It seems to me that you've always had someone, however unsatisfactory they may have been: your mother, your husband, this Alex. Couldn't you trust yourself a bit more? It takes a long time to make a life of one's own. You have to work at it, like marriage. But why don't you try it? Remember, you're so much luckier than most. You have the wherewithal and another priceless possession."

"You mean . . . my painting?"

"Yes. Look, stay here with us a little longer. You're doing fine. Think over what I've said. You can always go up to London for a day to see to anything if you want to."

It made sense, all of it. At the end of another week she wrote to Alex, and two days later went up to town to sign something for Mr Gregory and see an estate agent. It was as if, suddenly, she had been presented with the right path out of a maze. For once, there looked like being no dead ends. With Dr Cheriton's blessing, she could go on. The divorce was a mere formality. Apart from the necessity of her signature on a few papers, it was something quite automatic to be attended to by lawyers, interested parties far more connected with it than she herself. And if Hugh was chafing in the background, doing his best to stir them on to greater activity in order to make someone the second Mrs Brent, then he was welcome. The problem of where the first Mrs Brent was going to live presented more difficulties, but if Alex could absent himself for so long as he was now doing, he could hardly blame her for not wanting to remain in London alone. If he asked to rent the house from her she would have to be firm. It would be better if they did not meet, if the whole thing could be done by remote control, like the divorce. A sense of urgency came over her. She would get someone to come and look at her home, if possible that very day. She must act now, while she was still at St Margaretta's. She telephoned the firm of Marden and Major from the station, and was delighted when they promised to send someone along at 4 p.m.

Down in the Strand, even dry, case-hardened Mr Gregory complimented her on her appearance. "I'm so glad, Mrs Brent, to see you looking so much better. One never likes undertaking any divorce case when one's client is so obviously under the weather . . ."

The house was cool, rather dark, yet in no way oppressive when she let herself in during the early afternoon. But despite the fact that it was hers, that she had put so much of herself into it, there was, she reflected, still too much of Alex about the place to make her feel the owner. She supposed he would have received her letter by now. Surely he would understand? there must be other studios, other places to live. He would never be able to cope with the whole of this house by himself, anyway. Perhaps he would spend most of his time in Cornwall now. Go into semi-retirement. Simply rent somewhere to paint in London and live at a club whilst so doing.

Thinking of painting, she went up to her own small

room, drew back the curtains and pulled *Highline* out of
the cupboard. As soon as Vincent returned she would send
it to him as a gift. It would be the ideal present for all he had
done in helping her on the road to recovery. She placed it
against one wall and stood back. She was so busy studying
it, appraising it, that she heard no footsteps coming along
the passage behind her, only the words, "Not bad, Dishy,
not bad at all." She swung round to face Alex standing in
the doorway.

She backed away as he came forward, his eyes still
studiously contemplating the picture. "I always said you
had talent, my dear. Perhaps, in a quiet way, a spot of
genius. It's really," he stopped, and then, for the first time,
turned to her, "very good. Very good indeed."

She placed herself deliberately between *Highline* and
him. "Why have you come today, Alex? What are you
doing here?"

"I got your letter, of course. Whatever's got into you?
Wanting to sell this house. Silly Dishy. I never heard of
such a thing."

She took a step towards him, lifted her hand and brought
it hard across the side of his face.

"Oh dear. That was bad, my love. Very bad. I may have
been away longer than I meant, but that's no reason for you
to . . ."

She brought her other hand up to repeat the process but
he caught both of them quickly in his.

"It's no good, my dear. You know as well as I do that you
don't really want to get rid of this place. Or me." His arms
were encircling her now, his body hard against her own.
"This is where you belong, Dishy. Where I belong." His
mouth came fiercely down on hers. Then he began pushing
her, quite gently now, back towards the couch in a corner of
the room. Vincent, Dr Cheriton, St Margaretta's, even the
ringing of the doorbell by the representative from Marden
and Major stood no chance before what was about to take
place.

28

Apart from all the other regrettable things for which Sophie often felt Alex to be primarily responsible, was the fact that he had made—or she had allowed him to make—her rude and ungrateful. And what was more, rude and ungrateful to those people to whom she owed so much. Later that evening she simply telephoned St Margaretta's and left a message that she had been unavoidably detained in London. Then they went out to dinner, a dinner at which Alex's sense of fun, shamelessness and pleasure in the moment completely obliterated guilt, remorse and any feelings of obligation. She became happy and slightly high. There would be time enough to think up a letter of apology to Dr Cheriton in the morning.

Here, however, she was wrong. At 9 a.m., when they were still in bed, the telephone rang and a female voice said, "Mrs Brent?"

"Yes."

"This is Dr Cheriton's secretary here. Would you hold on one moment, please." Disconcertingly abrupt, Dr

Cheriton then came on the line.

"I understand that something kept you in London yesterday, Mrs Brent. I trust that it was nothing serious?"

"No. That is, I was just about to write to you."

"Does that mean you are not intending to return to St
Margaretta's today, Mrs Brent? You're still a patient here,
remember."

"Yes, but I . . ." She paused, trying to collect her
thoughts, a pause which was long enough to give rise to an
interjection more abrupt, more accusatory.

"You are trying to tell me, I think, that for reasons which I
can, of course, only guess at, you have decided to abandon
our treatment."

"Yes."

"Your decision has something to do with Mr Dolan, I take
it?"

"Yes."

"Mrs Brent, I cannot compel you to return, but I think
you are making a grave mistake. I also think Mr Matheson
will be extremely disappointed."

"Yes, I realise that."

"You understand that if you don't come back here, it will
be impossible for me to help you further should you need
it."

"Yes."

"Then will you think it over for an hour or so? If I do not
hear from you by, say, eleven o'clock, I shall know that we
have failed. There is no need to write."

Alex had remained silent while she was speaking, something he did not always do, occasionally tickling her or
muttering under his breath when she was trying to be
serious. As soon as she put down the receiver, he stretched
out an arm and drew her to him.

"Poor Dishy. You must have had a jailer in that ghastly
place."

"No. She was trying to help. I happened to be in a bad
way."

"I'm sorry. I won't abandon you again. I promise. But
you must admit that my own particular brand of restorative
treatment is faster acting than any which that female dragon

on the end of the line could dole out."

She did not say: but for you I would never need such
treatment, but for you I would never have experienced the
extreme limits of all the most destructive emotions:
jealousy, depression, despair, loneliness. For she was
aware that because of him, she had also known counter-
balancing extremes, one towards which Alex was urging
her this very moment. Both of them knew there would be
no question of ringing Dr Cheriton before eleven.

Autumn came early that year. A few weeks later, with a
shock, she noticed leaves being swept up in the gardens
below, woollen-clad children being hurried to school, fewer
people taking advantage of the seats beneath the sycamore
trees. Alex, for once, was as good as his word. After his long
absence he threw himself into work with renewed, almost
feverish, enthusiasm. In between times, he was loving,
considerate and everything for which she could have
wished. If he had initially been lured back by the thought of
losing his home rather than his home-keeper, she allowed
herself the satisfaction of believing that she mattered to him
a great deal more than he realised or would ever admit.
There was so much of the child about him. After a bad bout
of influenza to which he succumbed in early October, a
certain motherliness became more apparent in her attitude
towards him.

The decree nisi of her divorce case passed almost unnoticed, neither she nor Hugh having to go to court. By
Christmas, as he had wished, he would be free to remarry.
She felt nothing, save occasional astonishment that so
comparatively long a marriage could have faded into such
total oblivion. Could she really have spent all those years
with another human being and, with him, actually produced a third human being? Was she a cold-blooded
monster to feel so detached about it? Surely it ought to mean
something? Even Jamie sometimes seemed a chimera, disconnected as much in body as in distance. What had
happened? What had come over her? She seemed to have
changed out of all recognition: the way she wore her hair,
her make-up, her fashionable and, of late, somewhat outré,
provocative clothes. Even Alex had raised an eyebrow

when she appeared in an evening dress she had just purchased, which had a particularly plunging neckline. A year
ago she would never have dared to go out with him wearing
it. Now, she not only did not mind, but, in her wilder
moments, experienced a definite desire to shock, a pleasure
in defiantly acting out her improbable, out-of-keeping role.

Only one thing kept nagging at her conscience: Vincent.
He must have returned from France by now and she knew
she ought to get in touch with him. He had sometimes
telephoned while she was at St Margaretta's. He would
obviously have rung again and been told that she had left.
His very silence was enough to tell her that he knew, or had
guessed, what had happened.

One day, in a mood half penitent, half capricious, she
called to see him, hoping he might possibly be out and she
could drop a note through the letter-box. His home was not
far from hers and she went on foot, having abandoned the
idea of presenting him with *Highline* for the time being.
Under the circumstances, it hardly seemed appropriate
and, in any case, Alex's approbation had made her change
her mind.

There was no escaping Vincent for he came to the door
himself, thinner, deeply tanned, his eyes briefly lighting up
with pleasure before a guarded look came into them.

"Hello, Sophie."

"Hello, Vincent." She paused. Then her new-found self-
possession re-asserted itself. "Aren't you going to ask me
in?"

"Of course." He stepped aside. His house, as usual, was
immaculate. She had forgotten what an incredibly tidy and
organised person he was. "Come into the library. Would
you like some tea?"

It had not long gone three o'clock. She had purposely
chosen a time when she hoped he would not feel obliged to
offer her anything, certainly not a drink.

"No thank you. I just felt, well, I owed you some sort of
explanation. You were very kind, Vincent."

Before replying, he seemed to study her carefully. She
felt that she might have been a patient of his and supposed,
in a way, she was.

"I hoped . . . I might have helped. You don't need to apologise. I gathered what must have happened. You look remarkably well, my dear. At the moment."

She was sorry he added the last three words. They hung between them, like a challenge, as if he were deliberately reminding or warning her of a possibility she did not wish to contemplate.

"I'm learning to live in the present, Vincent. Like Alex. It's the only way. Please don't spoil it. It's working out. I'm . . . happy."

"I'm glad, Sophie. You may not believe this, but I should like to feel you were being appreciated. Perhaps Alex realises at last . . ." He broke off and dropped his gaze.

"Will you come to dinner with us sometime, Vincent? We'd like that very much. Alex was only saying the other day that it was time we saw something of you again. How about next Saturday?" She was being bright, purposely bright. She wished he wasn't so *nice*, that he didn't love her the way he did. She wondered what it would be like to go to bed with him. With her liberalizing experience of the past two years, would she shock him? Suddenly she wanted to shock him, to tell him what fun it was and she had to have it and that was why she was still with Alex. I'm doing all right, Vincent, she wanted to shout. All right, do you hear?

He looked up at her again steadily. "I'm afraid I shall be away at the weekend, Sophie. But thank you, all the same. Some other time perhaps."

Was he really going away? She wondered about it all the way home. For all his many friends, she knew he was still a lonely man. She had absolutely no grounds for thinking this, but it crossed her mind that perhaps he was thinking of marrying one of them.

29

She had been looking forward to Christmas this year. Cara or no Cara, she was determined that it should not be the travesty of the last. "If you were nice and welcoming, Dishy," Alex said, "I suppose she might just come to London. But I doubt it. Let's go down to Tremarthen early and do our best."

When Sophie was alone the next day she took the initiative and telephoned the other woman. For a moment she thought she detected signs of wavering, but then the voice on the end of the line took on its usual cryptic defensiveness. "I think not, Sophie, thank you all the same. I'll open up the house and get things ready before you come. I shall naturally like to see something of you both, but please don't imagine I shall be round your necks all the time."

After she rang off Sophie sat by the telephone half angry, half wondering, at Cara's strange mentality. Could she herself, given the same circumstances, have possibly behaved in such a way? Preparing a house for a man one loved who was about to inhabit it with another woman?

Would she have hung on, accepting whatever corner of Alex he was prepared to give her? The answer was 'no'. The situation was beyond her, the personalities involved too complex. Moreover, she did not want Tremarthen got ready for her by anyone else. She would prefer to do the 'opening up' herself, even if it did mean the bed was not exactly aired, no food in the refrigerator. What was the matter with this woman, emotionally blackmailing a man who had once, though long ago—or so Sophie had been given to understand—been her lover? Yet what was it like to have been beautiful, presumably adored, and now so handicapped? Did she herself lack compassion? And anyway, wasn't she hooked enough on Alex so that she, too, was willing to put up with the most cavalier treatment as long as he wasn't unfaithful?

Unfaithful. The word brought one train of thought abruptly to an end and ushered in another even more unwelcome. Supposing Alex were unfaithful, had already been unfaithful? Or did the word only apply to the married? Something bandied about by lawyers in divorce courts? If one chose simply to live with a man, to have, as it were, a looser kind of relationship, perhaps one should not expect faithfulness thrown in with so tenuous a bargain. God knew Alex liked pretty women, and they liked him. He had had plenty of opportunity for succumbing to their advances and vice versa. She hardly thought it possible that he could still be attracted to Cara in that way, not now, not with all her afflictions, although she had sometimes speculated on just how much Cara had been able to conceal from him throughout the years. But what about his vivacious new customer, the one with the four children whom he was painting at this very moment? Who were his so-called friends in Lausanne whom he had visited earlier in the year after his wife's death? Where was he of an afternoon when he didn't return until five or six? She had often wondered, had once or twice made tentative enquiries, but his obvious distaste of direct questioning of any sort had prevented her from persisting, that, and a more or less unconscious desire not to know. She supposed she was a fool. She knew he couldn't be relied on to speak the truth.

And yet, when things were going well, when they seemed so close as, for instance, just now, infidelity seemed hardly possible. He was such a strange mixture. His feelings of obligation to the past were, if looked at dispassionately, commendable. After all, what had he got out of allowing two women to impose a seemingly inescapable duty on him? Was there anything Cara could give him now other than a constant nagging feeling of responsibility? Yet he wasn't the responsible type. What was it that bound them? Did Alex perhaps need the kind of sheet-anchor she provided, an escape, a cast-iron excuse for never becoming totally committed to anyone else? And, of course, at least to his face, uncritical devotion and admiration? She would never really know. She was too deeply within the maze to see anything clearly.

When the telephone rang later that evening and Alex said, "It's for you," she wondered whether, in fact, Cara had changed her mind, but it turned out to be a call which she had been half dreading, half expecting.

"Sophie?" The voice was almost unrecognisable in its quietness and total lack of emotion. "I thought you should know. George died today."

"Oh, my dear Liz."

"The funeral's Friday." There was a pause. "Katy's baby's due soon so they can't come back. I wondered . . ."

It was the first time Sophie could ever remember Elizabth so much as tentatively asking anything of her. She was glad afterwards that there had been not a moment's hesitation.

"I'll be there, Liz. Would you, perhaps, like me to come sooner. Tomorrow?"

"I'd like that very much, Sophie. Thanks." She hung up.

Alex looked at her over the top of his evening paper. It was not often that he took the trouble to be interested in her affairs. "Bad news?"

"George died."

"I'm sorry. Still, expected wasn't it?"

"It makes it no better. I'm going down, Alex. I've got to. She's all alone."

He shifted a little in his chair, his movement, the way he shook the paper somehow managing to convey disapproval. "Hasn't she got relatives?"

"An only daughter, heavily pregnant, in the United States. A brother in South Africa suffering from multiple sclerosis."

"Even so . . ." The paper rustled again accusingly. "It's hardly your responsibility, is it? We're meant to be going to Cornwall at the end of this week, remember?"

"Oh, for Christ's sake, Alex. What are friends for? What about your feelings for Cara?"

"That's rather different."

"Is it? Why?" Her voice rose. "Oh, I know you feel obligated. You hurt her and she suffered in a particularly unfortunate way because of it. And so you've dragged the thing out ever since, ruining the present, allowing her to make demands. All I'm trying to do is to help a very dear friend at a particularly bad time. It's not much to ask, Alex. I'm not suggesting we take on Liz for the rest of her days, telephone her at every twitch and turn, let her interfere with our life . . ." She was in full spate now, surprising even herself, a hot lava of resentment pouring out, her voice shriller, her whole body trembling. "You don't suppose, do you, that when Christmas comes round each year I shall ask you to stay with Elizabeth or vice versa? In any case, she's not the clinging type. Too many guts . . ."

She saw him rise and walk towards the door. Then he turned and faced her before leaving the room. "By all means spend Christmas with your friend. I will spend it with mine."

30

There were only six of them round the graveside, not count-
ing Mr Haynes, the vicar: Elizabeth, George's widower
brother, a long-haired nephew, two next-door neighbours
and Sophie.

Yet though relatives may have been in short supply, the
little village church had been packed for the ordinary,
simple service preceding the burial, George having had a
hatred of cremation. It was obvious that he had been, as
Elizabeth had said only the evening before, greatly loved;
and greatly loved, Sophie realised as never before, by one
person in particular: his widow.

At the end of the day, Elizabeth seemed to crumple, even
to shrink. Sophie had been shocked to find how much she
had aged during the past year. She had expected change,
been prepared for grief, but not for the sudden capitulation,
the meek acceptance of help, the inability to decide. One
could never tell, of course, how others would behave in any
given situation but from Elizabeth, always so bright, so
aware, so sensible, she had automatically assumed a totally

different reaction from the one with which she was now confronted.

Elizabeth was lost. George had been her *raison d'être*. In all their married life they had rarely been apart more than five days. Sophie remembered how Elizabeth while seeming to enjoy her little break in London, had nevertheless been anxious to return, aware that she was missed. "My Rock of Gibraltar gets a little distrait without me, Sophie." What, in heaven's name was his widow going to do without that rock?

For a few days Sophie did nothing other than respect Elizabeth's desire to be left alone, not burdened by questions or problems, although there were plenty to sort out. As far as possible, she took over the running of the house and removed the more obvious signs of George's presence. Old gumboots, mackintoshes, walking-sticks she relegated to a corner of an outhouse, letters addressed to him she decided to open and deal with if she could. In the afternoons, while Elizabeth was resting, she left the telephone off the hook. At other times she answered it herself. Her efforts, to some extent, kept her free from tormenting herself too much over Alex, although not even Liz's plight could totally remove the constant ache, the sudden surge of loneliness and anxiety when she got into bed each night, the memory of those devastating words uttered, it seemed, with such callousness, "By all means spend Christmas with your friend. I will spend it with mine."

That event was not far away now. Snow had been falling during the last twenty-four hours and the view from the windows had begun to take on a seasonal look. George's garden, in which he took such pride, lay cold and glistening. Was his delight in the earth, in all things natural, the reason why he had preferred an ordinary burial? She shivered slightly and made up the fire, wondering whether Elizabeth would like her tea taken up to her. There was no sound from above. The house seemed completely still, somehow withdrawn, as if grieving in its own way, not wishing to be disturbed. Tumper, George's retriever, came across the room silently and laid his head on her lap.

This was what it was to lose a genuine love, to mourn the

end of a real marriage. It wasn't like the vulgar bewailing of some lover at the break-up of an affair. There was something, however tragic, almost right and proper about this kind of parting. There was none of the acrimony, the mortification, the fault-finding that left the bitter taste. If one had to leave someone, surely it was better for it to be done by the process of dying than by living through divorce or some vitriolic slanging match. There was no failure or cause for remorse in the way George and Elizabeth had parted—only an infinite sadness in which love still seemed alive.

It was almost another week before Elizabeth seemed to become aware that Sophie was still there. It was a relief when she at last referred to the fact, not because Sophie wished to get away for, in any case, she had no clear idea where she wanted to get away to. But at least Elizabeth's remark showed that she was perhaps a little on the way to coming out of a state of shock.

"You must want to get back, Sophie. I've kept you too long. I'm afraid I had no idea . . ."

"Nonsense. I'll stay as long as you want me to."

"But Alex. He'll be missing you, needing you."

She looked away, clenching her hands together. *I must keep Alex out of this, I will not let Liz know. I've prepared my speech enough. This is one of those times when lying is not only necessary but right.*

"No need to worry about Alex at all. We agreed. Cara's ill and he's gone to look after her. In many ways it's even *convenient* my being here."

"But Christmas, Sophie."

"Makes no difference. I'm not leaving you over Christmas. God forbid. In any case, I don't really want to go to Cornwall."

"I'd be all right, you know. George's brother asked me there. And I've good neighbours."

"Forget it."

The ringing of the telephone suddenly interrupted their conversation and Sophie crossed the room to answer it. The call was from New York. As clear as if he were in the next room she heard Elizabeth's son-in-law announcing the premature but safe arrival of her first grandson. "And we

would like her to come," the voice went on, "if she's up to
it. The sooner the better. Spend the rest of the winter with
us." Something like the old Elizabeth took the receiver
quickly out of her hands.

In the frantically busy days which followed, Sophie
couldn't help sometimes wondering fancifully if George
had had a hand in the timing. It was such a wonderful
solution. She watched Elizabeth get back almost, as it were,
into gear again, albeit a gentler, more subdued Liz, often
pensive, yet going through each day with a purpose.
"Thank God I've got a visa. You see although I knew he'd
never be able to make it, George and I sometimes used to
talk about going out there later on after the baby was born
and I thought, well, to make it seem more likely, something
for him to look forward to, I'd see to that side of things
early. I suppose it's a bit of a risk leaving the house at this
time of the year but the Barringtons next door are wonderful. And my daily will keep an eye on it, too. And poor
Tumper. I know she'll have him. I wonder . . ." Her voice
trailed away.

"You're wondering if you might live out there?"

"How did you know?"

"Oh, just guessed. I've thought about it quite a bit."

"Well, one thing's for sure. If I do set up home in
America, you—and Alex if he'll come—must be my first
visitors. Oh God, fancy talking about setting up another
home so soon after . . . George."

"I'm glad you can. So would he be. And he'd be so
pleased about the baby, Liz. Life, well, going on, somehow.
A new birth seems to make it, oh, I don't know . . ."

"You're thinking of Wordsworth, aren't you? 'Our birth
is but a sleep and a forgetting . . .' trailing clouds of glory
and all that. I don't suppose you thought I was so much of a
poetry reader?"

Elizabeth flew from Heathrow two days before
Christmas. Just before she went through into the departure
lounge, she said awkwardly, "I'm so damn bad at this sort
of thing, Sophie. Just saying thank you seems so inadequate. I'd never have got by alone. I thought perhaps you
might like this." She produced a book from one of her

voluminous bags. "George was always very fond of it. It's quite a rare edition. Flowers. Beautifully illustrated. I know he'd like you to have it. Now just you go back to Alex and be nice to him. Have a happy Christmas, Cara or no Cara."

Then she was on her way, a large rangy figure, carrying a strange assortment of paraphernalia. She stopped once, turned and waved over the top of a man wearing a fez. Only when she had quite disappeared did the other faces around Sophie seem to blur, so that it was all she could do to get herself safely down the moving staircase.

31

The Cornish express was crowded. Although travelling first class, she had only just managed to get a seat, unfortunately not in a non-smoker. Even at the beginning of the journey, the carriage seemed stuffy and full of fumes. She was also uncomfortably aware of a pricking in her throat signifying an on-coming cold.

To go to Tremarthen on Christmas Eve had been a spur of the moment decision, partly to do with Elizabeth's last words, partly because there suddenly seemed no alternative. For the idea of spending Christmas by herself in London was too abhorrent to contemplate. Apart from the main shopping areas, the capital was already beginning to take on a deserted look. In the smaller streets and squares cars were being loaded, whole families moving out. Everyone was going somewhere. Only she, Sophie Brent, divorced and loverless, seemed to be alone. She would have to do *something*. She would go to Cornwall. She decided to give no warning of her intentions, simply to arrive, as a *fait accompli*, around—or so she hoped—nine o'clock that night.

She had meant to read on the journey, but the atmosphere in the carriage, tiredness and an increasingly sore throat combined to produce a state of dull detachment. Occasionally she glanced out of the window wondering whether it was Exmoor or Dartmoor somewhere beyond the bleak, misty blankness through which the train seemed to be travelling at an astonishing speed. She wished she could summon up a modicum of the seasonal enthusiasm which the couple opposite her were showing. "I sometimes wish I'd bought Tom the smaller size," the wife was saying, to which her husband replied comfortingly, "Oh no, dear, I think you did quite right. He's big in the chest, you know." Who was Tom? Son, son-in-law or grandson? What was it this woman had bought? Sweater, shirt, pyjamas? Sophie closed her eyes. Did it matter? Christmas, as far as she was concerned, seemed a disastrous time. She had rushed out that morning purchasing almost the first things which came to her notice, a pen for Alex, a silk scarf for Cara. It seemed churlish to arrive unannounced with nothing and yet, why should she have bothered? Presents would probably only cause embarrassment. Not knowing she was coming, they would have nothing for her.

At five o'clock she went along to the buffet car and bought herself a gin and tonic, which had little effect other than to make her feel more depressed and bemused. Yet she found herself buying a second and third before she got off the train at Penzance, having felt quite unable to face any food. The queue for taxis was long and she waited in an icy wind for one to return, having already deposited passengers from the same train. She was so relieved to get out of the cold that at first she did not take much notice of the young driver. Only when—after a certain amount of difficulty in explaining to him the whereabouts of Tremarthen—he shot away from the station as if embarking on some race, did she begin to regard the back of his dark, wavy-haired head with growing apprehension. When he slammed on the brakes at a certain crossing so that she was thrown forward against the front seat, she asked, somewhat tentatively, whether he would mind reducing speed, as she was in no particular hurry.

He leered round at her, a preponderance of white teeth showing in his heavy, saturnine face, breathing garlic into the confined atmosphere in which, despite her thankfulness for warmth, there appeared to be no ventilation. She judged him to be around thirty, of Italian origin.

"Frightened, Missus?"

"I prefer to go more slowly. That's all." She spoke coldly, yet hoping she had not antagonised him.

Her driver took his foot off the accelerator and slowed to an exaggerated degree. "'Course, if you'd sooner enjoy the scenery, Missus . . ."

She began to feel really frightened now. The effect of alcohol had worn off long ago. She found herself breaking out into a sweat which did not seem to be altogether due to the heat in the car or her indisposition. She wished he would not call her 'Missus' in such a disrespectful tone, although perhaps it was as well that he thought of her as that old. Now that they were going so slowly she was even more aware of the lonely night outside, the occasional deep, high-banked lanes, hemming them in until suddenly they were out in the open again, a watery moon illumining a vague impression of sea and sky and space.

"Staying wiv friends, eh Missus? Out at Tremarthen?"

"Yes."

"Pretty wild out there, in't it? Never been to the house before, but, come to think of it, I believe one of my pals went there once. Don't it belong to some artist chap?"

"Yes."

"Wouldn't like to spend Christmas there, myself. Still, there's no accountin' for taste. You a friend of his, I suppose?"

"Yes."

He leered round at her once more.

"Funny chaps, artists. By all accounts."

She ignored his remark and blew her nose, loudly.

"Got a cold have you, Missus? Not much fun at Christmastime. Bet it's none too warm out there. I like Penzance myself. Got a nice little heated place, down by the harbour."

Still she did not answer. Surely he could take a hint? He
had picked up speed again now and was beginning to drive
more reasonably. With any luck they would be at
Tremarthen within another quarter of an hour. Then, to her
horror, she saw one of his hands leave the steering wheel
and start foraging around in a front compartment of the
dashboard. The car swerved and he corrected it quickly
before continuing his search. What was he looking for? The
thought of a gun crossed her overwrought mind. Suddenly
his hand shot up, brandishing something white. "Have a
peppermint, Missus?"

She laughed a little, in relief. "No thank you."

"Good for that cold you've got coming on."

"No thank you. I shall be eating soon." She had never felt
less like eating, but it seemed as good a way as any of letting
him know she was definitely expected. "We turn off shortly,
towards the cliff."

"O.K. Gawd, it's lonely, in't it? Shouldn't care for this
part at all. Lot of funny things go on hereabouts, so they
say. Some house near here that no one ever stays in long.
Haunted. T'wouldn't be Tremarthen, would it, Missus?"

"No. Here's the turning."

He turned off and they bumped along the stony track for
half a mile. Anxiously she looked for the lights of
Tremarthen. Surely they would be visible by now? The
moon had gone behind a cloud and they seemed to be
plunging on towards the cliff's edge in total darkness.

"That it, Missus?" Suddenly the house lay before them,
black, gaunt, and strangely lifeless. Something else about it
seemed different, and then she noticed the roof, one end of
which appeared to be covered by a tarpaulin, flapping in the
wind. Ladders and workmen's paraphernalia lay on the
ground.

"Don't look as if anyone's here, do it?" Her companion
had run down his window and was staring up at the unwel-
coming sight. Panic-stricken, she had come to the same
conclusion. "Best make sure, though." He got out, making
no attempt to help her as she followed suit, simply walking
behind her as she went forward uncertainly, knowing that
any attempts at entry would be fruitless. Tremarthen was,

indeed, deserted, the defective roof to which Alex had sometimes referred being at last in the hands of builders. A feeling of utter frustration and anger came over her, temporarily overcoming her fear of her too-familiar companion. The wind came straight from the sea in squally gusts, rattling the tarpaulin and lifting her skirt beneath her shorter fur-lined suede jacket. She shivered and found an arm disconcertingly under her elbow.

"Best get back in the car, Missus."

"Yes."

She shook off his attentions, hating him witnessing her humiliation. Who, other than a fool, would be stranded like this on Christmas Eve?

He did not immediately close the door after she got into the back seat again and she made a movement to shut it herself. He leant forward quickly, thrusting his face at hers, his garlic-laden breath offensively close. "Reckon they can't be expecting you, Missus. What you gonna do?"

She summoned all the control she was able. "Mr Dolan did warn me about the roof. If Tremarthen was uninhabitable for Christmas he told me where to find him." It was a poor excuse and she knew he would have seen through it. Feverishly, she racked her mind for Cara's address. "Would you kindly drive me to . . . to Number Three, Coastguard Cottages, Porthconnon."

So swiftly that she could only stare in stupefied horror, she saw his right hand unzip the leather jerkin he was wearing, revealing his repulsively tight jeans beneath. Then she became aware that his hand was suddenly busy about his person again. She struck out at him blindly with both arms and, to her surprise, he fell back, hitting his head on the side of the car before he keeled over awkwardly, to the sound of swearing and broken glass.

He looked up at her, incredulously, from the ground. "Look what you've fucking done, Missus. There was no need to turn nasty like that. What do you take me for? You didn't think I was going to try anything on, did you? I thought you looked peaky and could have done with a drop of what's gone to the dogs."

She noticed blood on one of his hands and, for a wild

moment, wondered whether she had really hurt him. Then, to her relief, she watched him get up, wrap a handkerchief round what appeared to be only a slight cut and, somewhat sheepishly, get back into the driver's seat. She closed her own door and they set off in silence, the reek of his whisky-soaked clothes overcoming that of garlic. It was all she could do not to throw up on the journey for which, at the end, he asked for forty pounds.

She paid him the exact amount, picked up her suitcase, which he had more or less thrown down on the ground beside her, and walked up the short path towards a home she had never seen. But at least Alex's car was standing outside and there was a light in the downstair windows.

32

A look of undisguised hostility came over Cara's face when she saw the identity of her visitor. It was Alex who had opened the front door, which led straight into the living-room. A coal fire was burning in the grate and on a low table in front of it a game of Scrabble appeared to be in progress. To Sophie, the scene seemed surprisingly cosy and almost grotesquely domestic. She felt she had intruded on some long-established happily-married couple whom she had never seen before. She had certainly never associated Alex with Scrabble, had been unaware that he even knew there was such a game.

"Come and sit by the fire, my dear. Let me take your coat." He was uncertainly avuncular, trying to do his best in a delicate situation. Cara half rose and then sat down again suddenly, as if the effort was too much for her.

"I'm sorry to butt in like this. I had no idea about Tremarthen."

"You've been there?" Alex, still uneasy, pulled up another chair.

"Well, naturally. I took it for granted that's where I'd find you."

She saw him frown. "I'm afraid you must have had quite a journey. What can I get you?"

"Nothing, thanks."

"Surely, a drink? I believe there's some rum in the kitchen." He got up with a proprietary air, busying himself fetching bottles and glasses. Cara remained seated, staring, with unnecessary concentration, into the flames.

"Here, you look as though you need this." Alex passed her a glass and she did not demur, although her throbbing head and feeling of nausea had all but taken away her desire for alcohol.

"What happened to your friend?" Alex seemed to be speaking more out of a need to keep some conversation going rather than with any real interest.

"She went to the States yesterday."

"I see. Well, you did quite right to come. I only wish you'd let us know, that's all." The use of the word 'us' did not escape her.

Cara leant forward, making rather too elaborate a show of making up the fire. With her back still towards Sophie, she said, "The trouble is, I've only two bedrooms. I imagine we shall want one each?"

Sophie felt the situation slipping out of control. The rum, in her feverish state, had begun to make her feel not so much light-headed as queer. The three of them sitting there with so much constraint between them was almost farcical. In London she and Alex slept together, as Cara must very well know. Presumably, in Cornwall, she had to pretend they didn't, not that she would have wished to do anything of the sort under Cara's roof.

"No problems," she heard Alex saying, "I can sleep on the sofa."

"I don't see why you should." Cara was openly antagonistic now, like some angry bird protecting her young.

Sophie, her voice hoarse and seeming to come from somewhere else, said, "I can go to a hotel."

"For crying out loud!" Alex's hitherto controlled anger began to show. "We'll stay here tonight and tomorrow we'll go over to Tremarthen and see whether it wouldn't be possible to inhabit part of the house. All of us," he added, as an afterthought.

Cara drained her glass and held it out to Alex to be refilled, the two strawberry-red spots on her cheek-bones telling more than her actual words. "Count me out, Alex. I always said I shouldn't be round your necks. Now that Sophie has elected to come for Christmas after all, you must both enjoy it in your own way. Although, judging by the look of her, it would seem she might have to spend it in bed—alone."

It was Alex who flushed now. He turned on Cara, his whole face distorted with an anger Sophie had seldom seen. "You bloody well stop being such a bitch. I've allowed you to ruin my life long enough. I've done my best. You can spend Christmas by yourself and be as miserable as you damn well want."

Sophie closed her eyes. Did he always have to have a scapegoat? Sometimes it seemed to be her turn, sometimes others. She should never have come. Better to have stayed in London nursing whatever malaise she seemed to have. Sometimes when one was physically ill, mental distress was easier to bear. One was too busy keeping warm or cool or trying to relieve a stomach-ache to bother about emotional bruises. The immediate urgency of some bodily pain was an anodyne.

She was hardly aware of Cara's departure from the room, only a welcome silence apart from the noise of the wind and an occasional splutter from the grate. Presently, she looked across to where Alex was sitting, his head in his hands. "I shouldn't have said it," he said, at length. "I shouldn't have said it."

"And I shouldn't have come." She had difficulty in speaking now and her voice was no more than a whisper, so that she was unsure whether he had even heard. They sat on in a kind of hopeless inertia in which she lost count of time. She scarcely registered that he had left her until she noticed him standing in the doorway.

"She's gone out. She does that sometimes, when she's piqued. God knows how long she'll be."

"It's not a very good night for walking." She remembered the wind around Tremarthen.

"That wouldn't worry Cara. In fact," he laughed, shortly, "I've sometimes called her my 'foul-weather friend'."

She got up unsteadily and went across to him. "I'm sorry, Alex. I shouldn't have spoiled it. She's upset. As I said, I should never have come."

"Of course you should have come. I wanted so much for you to come. Why else do you think I was so annoyed when you said you couldn't? I don't want Cara to feel that she has the right to, well, dictate my Christmases."

"Yet you seemed so happy together, when I arrived."

"God, I've told you. I make the best of things now. I make do. Surely you must have realised long ago that my life is one hell of a mess. Always has been."

She did not answer. She simply felt an urgent need to lie down. Presently she said, "Alex, I'm awfully sorry. I must go to bed. Anywhere."

"Of course. Forgive me. You won't, I take it, mind my sheets? Incidentally, the bathroom's downstairs."

He picked up her suitcase and led the way. The cottage was even smaller than she had imagined and it seemed as if the only bedrooms were almost intercommunicating. He gathered up a few of his belongings, including Hob who had been sitting somewhat forlornly on the bedside table, placed a brief kiss on her forehead and, with a "I'll be in the sitting-room if you want anything," wished her good-night.

At three a.m. she woke with a start, cold, shivering and almost unable to swallow. Staggering downstairs to the bathroom she noticed the door of Cara's bedroom still wide open and the bed not slept in. Surely she couldn't be still out walking? The sitting-room also appeared to be empty. Had Alex gone out too, presumably looking for her? She was reminded of the previous time when she had been staying at Tremarthen and, with variations, this seemed like a repeat performance. Did coming to Cornwall always mean that someone made some sort of dramatic exit? Were the three of them, between them, compelled to act out a bizarre tragedy on a stage which simply waited for the play to begin? With infinite sadness, she remembered it was

Christmas Day.

She switched on an electric heater and, for a while, sat huddled by the fire, trying to revive its dying embers, until the front door suddenly opened and brought her to her feet. Alex stood there, enveloped in oil-skins and sou'-wester, looking for all the world like a member of some life-boat crew. She went towards him and then something in his face made her stop.

"Cara not back?"

"No."

"If she doesn't turn up by the time it starts to get light I'll have to ring the police."

"The *police*?"

"There'll have to be a search. Not much good in the dark. I've tried some of her favourite haunts. She hasn't taken her car or mine, so she must be on foot."

"Has she ever done this sort of thing before?"

"Yes. But never for as long as this. And not on such a filthy night."

She made an effort. "Would you like a hot drink or something?"

"Stay where you are. I'll see to it." She sat down again, waiting miserably while he went into the kitchen, finally returning with two steaming mugs. Once again, his unsuspected domesticity surprised her. "There you are. Hot toddies."

They drank in silence, save for the merciless shrieking of the wind as it tore against the little row of cottages, beating at doors and windows, rattling latches and fastenings as if with human hands. Once, the front door actually burst open and Alex started up. "Cara?" But there was no sign of her, only a gaping blackness in which all the Furies seemed to be raging.

Alex made her go back to bed and she did so thankfully, although it was all she could do to climb the stairs. Through a half-sleep she thought she heard him telephone from time to time and then the door open and shut as he went out again.

33

Alex was out until darkness fell on Christmas Day and went off as soon as it was light the following morning. Throughout this time she remained, hot and helpless, in bed, the business of getting downstairs to the bathroom and back an ordeal in itself. When it got to six o'clock on Boxing Day and he still had not returned, anxiety forced her to get up once more and go into Cara's room to telephone the police station. The voice which answered asked her what relation she was to Mrs Lomax and Mr Dolan. It was quite a shock to hear Cara referred to by anything other than her Christian name.

"I'm a friend. Of them both." That was, perhaps, both an over and understatement, but there seemed nothing else to say. "I'm staying in Mrs Lomax's house."

"Ah, I see. Would you hold on, please."

To her relief, Alex himself answered the telephone. "I'll be late, Sophie, I'm afraid."

"Have you, have they ‵. . ?"

He cut her short. "I'll be back as soon as I can."

He arrived at nine o'clock, grey and exhausted. As if she had not already guessed, she was certain at once, even from where she was standing on the stairs, what had happened.

"Her body . . . washed up . . . late this afternoon. There'll have to be an inquest, of course."

"Oh, *no* . . ." She held on to the banisters and then walked slowly down to meet him. "Intentional? Was it intentional?"

"I imagine so. She could have fallen, I suppose. Go back to bed, will you? I'm all in."

She wanted to get close to him, feel his arms around her, have him tell her it was all some ghastly mistake, that it hadn't happened, that it had nothing to do with her anyway. Could they not at least find mutual comfort in the face of mutual suffering? Yet he was, in this hour of her need for him, as strange as a stranger. She went back upstairs, her mind heavy with guilt, her body weakened by fever. By her unpremeditated actions another human being had died, a human being who had already suffered more than most.

When the inquest took place to which Alex had referred, she was still hardly fit enough to attend. "I'd hoped it wouldn't be necessary for you to come, Sophie. If you hadn't happened to telephone the police that evening, you might never have been called."

She became impatient with him. "Inquests are to find out facts, aren't they? I'm a fact. A fact of the matter in question."

Disconcerted by her unaccustomed acerbity, he shrugged and opened the car door for her.

The coroner was a grey, pernickety little man who reminded her of her divorce lawyer, Mr Gregory. She wondered whether all men whose job it was to interrogate people had the same mien: apparent self-effacement, coupled with an ability to become suddenly galvanised into rapier-like activity, thrusting poison darts into their victims. When it came to her turn to speak, she did her best to control a surge of violent antagonism both towards him and the circumstances in which she found herself.

"You knew the deceased, Mrs Brent?"

"Yes."

"How long had you known her?"

She hesitated. She had known so much about Cara for longer than she had actually known her. "I first met her just under eighteen months ago."

"And she became a friend of yours?"

Again she hesitated. "An acquaintance would perhaps be more correct. I never knew her well."

The coroner looked down at his notes. "During your telephone call to Sergeant Blaydon on Boxing Day, I see you actually described yourself as a friend."

"Well, yes. It hardly seemed the time to go into technicalities. I was extremely anxious."

"About Mrs Lomax or Mr Dolan?"

"About both of them."

"Mrs Brent, was there anything prior to Mrs Lomax's disappearance which gave you reason to believe that she might take her own life?"

"It never occurred to me—until she was missing."

"And what gave you the thought that she might be responsible for her own death?"

"I knew she was upset."

"About what, Mrs Brent?"

There was an almost audible hush in the little court room now. She gripped the side of the small square enclosure she was in with one hand and took a sip of water with the other.

"Me. I arrived unexpectedly that night from London."

"Was that not a rather unusual thing to do? Most people make preparations for Christmas well in advance."

"There were exceptional circumstances. I had originally been going to spend Christmas with . . . with Mr Dolan. It was not until the last minute that I found myself able to do so."

"What you are inferring, Mrs Brent, is that Mrs Lomax was also hoping to spend Christmas with Mr Dolan and your sudden appearance distressed her?"

"Yes."

"Thank you, Mrs Brent."

34

It was not the memory of the hostile Cara whom she had last seen which now seemed forever with Sophie, but the shocking image of the woman who had once snatched off her wig and dark glasses in the kitchen at Tremarthen. That picture haunted her during all the hours of daylight and remained throughout every sleepless night. The fact that, in the face of inconclusive evidence, a verdict not of suicide but misadventure was brought in, made no difference. She longed to talk about it with Alex but he maintained a complete silence on the subject. Back in London, she retreated more and more into her little private quarters and at meals, which she found an increasing trouble to prepare, they rarely spoke. Once, after an estate agent had happened to telephone from Penzance, he informed her that he had put Tremarthen, despite being under repair, up for sale because he had no wish ever to go there again. She wondered what had happened about Cara's cottage but his manner made it all too obvious that he did not wish to discuss such matters further. Locked in their own separate desolation, the one bodily comfort which might have brought them nearer to achieving mental relief failed to take place.

And then one night, after such a state of affairs had been going on for well over two months, Alex suddenly appeared in her room when she was lying in bed trying to read.

"Sophie. Are you going to let Cara live with us for always?"

She put down her book and stared at him. He looked old, haggard. She knew that he had been suffering in his own way probably as much as she.

"I can't get her out of my mind, Alex."

"I don't suppose either of us will ever do that altogether."

"She seems sometimes more with us than when she was alive."

He came across and sat on the end of her bed. "I know you found it hard to accept her when she was. But she's dead now Sophie. We've got to go on. Somehow." He moved forward and she suddenly realised, in horror, what he had come for. Never, throughout their whole association, had she ever imagined there would come a time when she did not want him to touch her or make love to her.

"Alex, please. I can't. Not now. I may feel differently in a little while."

He swore, got up quickly and left her without another word.

When, a few days later, Elizabeth returned from the States, she was glad of an excuse to get away. "I've made arrangements with Mrs Tuffnell to come in more often, Alex. If you want her to come back and get you an evening meal, you've only to let her know."

He was painfully polite. "No thank you. I shall go out."

There was a time when she would have been disturbed, have wondered where he would be going. Now, their parting seemed to take place with mutual relief.

She found Elizabeth even more aged, yet calm and full of quiet resolve. "I'm going to do exactly what you thought, Sophie. I've even earmarked the place I want to live in over there. Katy's husband's tying up all the ends for me and I've just got to wind up over here. I shouldn't think this house will be too difficult to sell, spring coming on and all that. Incidentally, my dear, you don't look too good. Is everything all right?"

"Not exactly, but we won't go into it now."

Elizabeth gave her a long look. "I do wish things could go a bit smoother for you. Has Cornish Cara got under your skin again?"

"Cara is dead."

"*Dead?*"

"Please, Liz. Don't let's talk about it now. Not on my first night. Show me some photographs of your grandson. You must have some."

She stayed with Elizabeth for three weeks, helping to pack up while she put the house on the market. Sad though the situation was, the feeling of working for something worthwhile, a mutual appreciation of each other's company, the relief of not having to cope with Alex's unpredictable moods, made the time pass all to quickly. It was Elizabeth who brought up the latter subject one evening while they were finishing turning out the attics.

"I can't believe you've been here so long, Sophie."

"Nor can I."

"Have you heard from Alex?"

"No."

"Look, my love, I don't want to interfere, but if you're intending to remain with him, much as I shall miss your invaluable assistance, don't you think it's time you went to see how he's getting on? In any case, I shan't be here all that much more now."

"I expect you're right. I've just tried to put him out of my mind."

"But not Cara?"

"I suppose both, in their different ways, will always be with me. Yes, Liz, I'll go back tomorrow, if you're sure you can manage. One can't run away for ever."

Suddenly and unaccountably she wanted him again. After all, he had made the first overture. It was her turn now. Surely there must be a way, a formula for living together. After all, his two millstones, as far as she was concerned, were gone. It was wrong, as he had said, to allow the dead weight of one of them to transfer itself to her own neck. She would learn to accept and not expect. Life without him was unthinkable.

She arrived at the house at about three o'clock the following afternoon. Alex's car was outside but that did not necessarily mean he was at home, for he rarely took it on short journeys in London. The hall, on entering, had that certain neglected appearance which she had come to associate with Mrs Tuffnell's somewhat erratic flick of her duster whenever left to her own devices. It was all very silent and she imagined she was alone. It was not until she was almost outside the door where she and Alex usually slept that she heard a low murmur of voices, one Alex's, the other an unknown female one. She put down the suitcase she was carrying and stood absolutely still. There was a sudden rustling of bedclothes, a light laugh and then, "Alex Darling, how shall we manage all this if and when Sophie comes back?"

35

Vincent appeared to take her sudden appearance on his doorstep, together with her suitcase, quite calmly. He simply said, "Come in, Sophie. I'm afraid you've caught me in rather a mess."

He was, in fact, in an uncustomary state of disorder, wearing shirt sleeves and old trousers and surrounded by packing cases, although she registered little of this. She was only aware of having stumbled downstairs and out of the house and throwing herself into the first taxi which came along. When the driver had asked her where she wanted to go she had just given him Vincent's address, as if someone else had told her to do so. If anything, she was perhaps more surprised than he, when she found herself where she was.

"Come in the kitchen. There's still a chair or two there."

She sat down obediently and watched him fill the kettle while continuing, "I was dying for some tea. Glad you've given me an excuse to stop work and make a pot."

Presently he said, "I've made it good and strong. I don't

normally take sugar myself, although I sometimes find it
reviving on certain occasions. Will you have some?"

She nodded, dumbly, and watched him heap two large
spoonfuls into the cup before passing it to her. His matter-
of-factness, the quiet way he had accepted her obvious
distress, began taking away just a little of her immediate
feeling of sickness and shock. Like some animal in pain who
unconsciously turns to the right natural remedy, she had,
just as unconsciously, turned to Vincent. He asked her no
questions. He merely set about being enormously practical
regarding her immediate need for refuge and his own
ability to supply it. He conducted the somewhat one-sided
conversation in a desultory, unemotional manner, as if he
were briefing some old friend with necessary information
since their last meeting.

"I've been camping here, Sophie, as you can see. I've
bought a villa halfway up the mountains behind Menton.
You remember I was staying there last year and fell in love
with the Gorbio valley. There seemed nothing to keep me in
London now. Hence this move. But I know there's still a
camp bed somewhere about, so if you don't mind rather
slumming it, I suggest we put it up in the drawing-room
tonight and you can sleep there."

"Thank you, Vincent."

"Fine. That's settled, then. I shall like a little company.
My couple, Mr and Mrs Morgan, had the offer of such a
good job that I insisted they went off last week. They'd seen
me through the worst of all this, bless them, and I'm just
seeing to the rest. Attached as we all were to each other, I
knew they didn't relish the thought of coming to France
and, in any case, the villa is quite small. I intend to live fairly
simply and I've got a French girl who's prepared to come in
daily. Another cup?"

"Thank you."

The telephone rang and he got up to answer it, afterwards pottering quietly about the house again and, once,
pausing as he passed the open door with, "I've found the
bed and am putting it up now, in case you'd like to lie
down."

She thanked him again but remained where she was,

staring blankly out at the little courtyard at the back of the house, grey-green and desolate in the failing light. Later— she was unsure how long—he came back into the kitchen and, with extraordinary efficiency, produced some scrambled eggs. She became suddenly aware, as if someone had switched on a mechanism which had temporarily stopped working inside her, of his long, delicate hands as he stirred the saucepan, his finely-drawn features, the way in which, despite present difficulties, he had laid the table in as attractive a way as possible. Only when he had passed her a plate and sat down himself did he say, perhaps sensing that it would be easier while she was busy with her eyes and hands, "Tell me." He did not, as some people might have said, "Tell me if you want to." Yet he was not dictatorial. He spoke, perhaps, with quiet authority, the doctor in him knowing that this was the right time to operate.

She began to speak, haltingly at first, not just about her latest experience, but going back to the beginning, to Hugh, to Jamie, even her upbringing. They must have sat there at the kitchen table two or three hours. Sometimes, when she found it difficult to go on, he asked a small question or got up to make some more coffee. Only when she had told him of the events of that afternoon, did he say, "Poor Sophie," and get up to wash the dishes. This time she rose to help him also, the relief of what amounted to a confession reactivating her normal good manners.

"I'm afraid I've interrupted all your packing, Vincent. When are you leaving?"

He was silent for so long that she turned off the tap, wondering whether the noise of the water had prevented him from hearing her.

"I *was* going next week."

She turned towards him. The emphasis on the 'was' had not escaped her.

"Vincent, you mustn't delay because of me. Please. I shall be all right now."

He put down the tea-towel he was holding and placed an arm on each of her shoulders.

"Sophie, I asked you once before, remember, to come to

France with me and you refused. I'm asking you again now." And while she remained staring at him he added, "Although there is one small technicality that has to be overcome first. Tomorrow I'd like to see about getting a special licence."

36

She was shocked at Alex's appearance on the evening she
came to say goodbye to him. She found him in the studio,
unshaven, unkempt, a look of hopelessness in his eyes
which she did her best to ignore. It hardly seemed possible
that it was still less than two weeks since she had fled down
the stairs of this very same house and, metaphorically at
least, into Vincent's arms. Was she that much of a weakling,
a change-coat, a woman with no stronger feeling than that
of leaning on the first shoulder which offered itself? She
understood well now what it meant when people talked
about being 'caught on the rebound'.

She had done her best to be honest with Vincent after his
strangely assertive proposal. But was honesty enough? She
remembered their conversation:

"I don't feel . . . I mean, I'm not in love, Vincent."

"I've never felt being in love an absolutely necessary
condition for marriage, Sophie. An affair, yes. Time was
when marriages went very much better when the parties
involved did not start out in what I believe is sometimes

referred to as a state of madness."

She felt it had to be said. "But you are in love with me."

He had looked at her very steadily and she remembered thinking how she had never seen anyone with such blue eyes, nor anyone whose face seemed so totally without guile.

"Well, yes. I've been in love with you ever since you opened the door to me when I first came to sit for Alex. Beauty and unhappiness have always had powerful effects on me."

"Was I obviously so unhappy then?"

"I thought so."

"You weren't particularly concerned with character evidently. I don't think much of myself, you know."

"I know that and it seems a pity. I wish you did. You've got so much potential. If only you'd paint, as I hope you will, perhaps you would be able to come to easier terms with yourself."

"But how would painting tie up with looking after you, being your wife?"

"I'm not particularly demanding, Sophie. I don't want to be waited on. In France I believe you'd find the sort of milieu you need. As you know, I once thought of dabbling about with art myself, but I'm nowhere in your class. I know I'd get a much better kick out of helping someone with your kind of talent to realise it."

Put the way Vincent put it, the whole concept seemed faultless. He was holding the door open. She had only to walk through it. But what had she got to give him? Dispassionately, almost idly, she wondered whether sex would come into it. He had never referred to it, had made no overtures in that direction, had, in fact, behaved with unnaturally scrupulous propriety while she had been staying with him. Was he, perhaps, past sex? She knew men varied so much over the age when they gave it up or, rather, vice versa. There could be few to have retained their virility like Alex. Perhaps Vincent had never been the passionate type, able to manage without, especially now. Yet he certainly looked a far fitter specimen than Alex. His figure was astonishly lean and youthful. Supposing he said, 'Let's go to bed', would she be able to comply? Would it work? She was appalled at how cold-blooded she seemed to be about the whole proposition. She might have been considering the relative advantages of a prospective house or the comfort of a new mattress.

"It could," she had said at length, "be a very one-sided bargain, Vincent."

"That is for me to judge."

And because the words of her acceptance—a simple "All right"—had seemed so unromantic and ungracious, she had added, just before he came across the room to kiss her, "Thank you." Afterwards she felt that the whole incident had somehow taken place out of context, an Edwardian or Victorian transaction in which, though her hand had been sought and granted, it was now necessary to obtain the consent of some older person, a father perhaps or, in this case, Alex.

Vincent had wanted her merely to write to Alex only, but she had pointed out that they would also have to meet. For one thing, there was the question of the house, her personal possessions to remove and, although she scarcely wished to admit it, she wanted to prove something to herself and, indirectly, to Vincent. She wanted him to trust her. She wanted to trust herself.

As soon as she saw Alex she knew it was going to be a great deal more difficult than she had even imagined. His dejection seemed genuine, his apology prompt, surprising and sincere.

"I'm sorry, Sophie. In all our association I've never had sex with anyone else before. You can believe me or not, as you will. Anyway, it's over. It meant nothing. You did, you know, refuse me yourself."

"I was upset."

"You've been upset before."

"This was different."

"And now, according to your letter, you are proposing to leave me, for good."

"Yes."

"And go off with Vincent."

"Not 'go off'. We're about to be married."

"*Really*? I *see*. Ever the gentleman, Vincent." A more sarcastic note had crept into his voice now.

"Won't you find it rather dull?"

"I don't see why."

He was suddenly more spirited, almost a wicked look in his eyes. "Does he really turn you on?"

She flushed.

"Come, Sophie. Don't tell me you don't *know*, you haven't *tried*."

"It's got nothing to do with you."

"But everything to do with you, my love. I don't want you to find you've made a mistake. Surely you've *experimented*."

"Alex. I didn't come here to talk about Vincent. I came here to see about my personal things and talk about the house."

"Ah, yes. The House. All the nasty material mechanics of the situation. Well, I've sold Tremarthen, very badly, I might add. But I can buy this from you if you wish."

"Yes, I do wish. I'd like to do it through an agent, if you don't mind. It would seem . . fairer."

"Of course."

Afraid that she had sounded over-businesslike and grasping, she added by way of explanation, "I shall be out of the country soon. We're going to live in France."

She looked away, aware that he was watching her carefully. Even as she got up and walked towards the door she knew that his eyes were on her and into them had come that look which, please God, she could at last resist.

"I think I shall like France very much, Alex. I want to pack up a few things now and then perhaps leave instructions with Mrs Tuffnell to do the rest."

She was surprised at the swiftness with which he forestalled her.

"Don't, Dishy. Please don't. We've had something very special, you and I. It's always been different—with you. I won't hurt you again. I promise."

He stood with his arms outstretched across the door, but for once he did not attempt to touch her. Afterwards she often wondered what would have happened if he had. Was he, at last, being unselfish, knowing how near she was to acquiescence? She had a sudden recollection of childhood fantasies when she was being driven by Olivia and they came to a fork in the road: 'Which way shall we go, Darling?' 'You choose, Mummy'. And so they had always gone Olivia's way because she, Sophie, did not want to feel responsible for some hypothetical accident. It wasn't, of course, quite the same. Then, there were no two men each beckoning her in different directions, one mad and bad and looking at this moment like a haunted scarecrow in need of a woman's care, the other wise and good and perfectly capable of looking after himself without the need of the wife she had promised to be.

Her voice, when she spoke at last, was firm but laboured, as if, although she had made up her mind which route to take, the effort of the journey might be too much for her.

"It's too late, Alex." And then, when she saw his look of utter desolation, noticed how the hand which he now passed across his forehead seemed to be shaking, she added, gently, "Of course, if you ever really needed me . . . I mean, if you were ill or anything, I'd come."

Ten minutes later, while she was putting some dresses into a suitcase, he came into the room carrying a small box which he held out to her. "You once asked me Dishy, if we ever broke up, whether you could keep Hob. I should like you to have him. Think of him as a wedding present."

Before she left the house, she pulled *Highline* out of its cupboard and, together with a postcard on which she simply scrawled "Alex", propped it against the passage wall outside her room.

37

She had been married to Vincent for over three years when
the telegram came. On the whole they had seemed good
years, rewarding ones. She felt that she had made him
happy—sometimes embarrassingly so—and if her own
happiness was derived chiefly from the paintings which,
under his auspices, she managed to achieve, she did her
best to conceal the fact.

She had never before encountered a man so willing to
defer to her wishes, except in one sphere: that of her work.
It was not that he interfered or prevented her in any way
from doing it—as had Hugh and Alex—indeed quite the
reverse. Often she felt that he had become a taskmaster:
"Sophie, it's nearly ten o'clock. Oughtn't I to drive you up
to Eze before it gets much hotter . . ?" "Sophie Darling, I
told Mildred Jackson that we couldn't go for drinks this
evening. I knew you wanted to finish your *Village
Square.*"

Occasionally she would remonstrate gently with him,
saying that she would not mind an excuse to knock off, or

suggesting that perhaps he might attend some party without her. Then he would remind her of the show in Paris on which they had both set such store, and also that nothing would induce him to go to Mildred Jackson's or anywhere else without her.

With the help of Ginette, the villa ran smoothly. The girl would arrive, having shopped in the market at Menton each morning, in time to produce fresh coffee and croissants, after which she would spend the morning cleaning, preparing a salad lunch and leaving their dinner, mostly also prepared, for Sophie to cook that evening. Vincent, she discovered, ate little and she found herself doing likewise, becoming even thinner yet certainly healthier and suntanned under this spartan new régime. They managed a walk most days and always a bathe throughout the summer and early autumn, although Vincent was apt to take more of such exercise, leaving her to get on with painting, and then greeting her after any temporary parting with such undisguised pleasure that she sometimes felt unable to refrain from teasing him about it.

"It's nice," she said once, when they were sitting high above the villa waiting for the sun to disappear suddenly over the mountains, "being so cherished. I don't know what I've done to deserve it."

"You deserve it all right. You're happy, aren't you, Darling? As long as you are, I am."

And she answered, while reflecting how strange it was that neither Hugh nor Alex had ever used that particular term of endearment to anything like the same extent when talking to her, "Yes, Vincent. How could I not be?"

But in bed that night, she thought about her answer and wondered whether she was not deceiving both him and herself. She was certainly delighted, even astonished, with the pictures steadily accumulating in the studio she had made at the back of the house. She was grateful for Vincent's company, their peaceful evenings together at the end of each day when there often seemed no need to talk, but simply to sit watching the lights come on in the distant harbour below them; she felt secure in the knowledge that he wouldn't suddenly get up and throw some tantrum, say he was going away, tell her that some other woman needed his attention. She knew she was the only one in Vincent's life. His devotion and support were absolute.

Yet even while she appreciated this, knew it to be necessary to her, the sheer responsibility of his love often weighed more heavily than she wanted. He was too kind, too unselfish, even in his lovemaking. There was nothing exactly wrong with it, except that it wasn't like Alex's. Although she had refused to answer the latter's pertinent questions on the subject, she would certainly have liked to "experiment" before marrying, had once or twice, rather to her surprise, found herself trying to bring this about. But Vincent had seemed so set on adhering to some old-fashioned code of behaviour, so determined to put her on a pedestal, that she ceased to bother, simply allowing herself the pleasure of being adored in a way no man had ever done before.

When, at the beginning of their marriage, she did not achieve an orgasm, she refused to allow it to worry her unduly, although once or twice she tried to simulate one, afterwards hating herself for so doing. She thought Vincent was probably unaware of her failure in this respect, although she couldn't be sure. They rarely discussed sex. It was something which seemed to happen quite pleasantly, mostly of an early morning before Ginette's arrival, by which time Vincent had shaved and was in a dressing-gown sitting on a chair, with the bedside table between them, ready to receive the breakfast tray which she brought in. But sometimes, when Sophie was alone, a fierce over-whelming ache to have Alex make love to her again would suddenly take over. She knew that to indulge this feeling was dangerous, wrong, and could only bring subsequent unhappiness and remorse. Yet the desire occasionally became so strong, the lack of physical satisfaction so great, that she would abandon whatever she was doing and give in, later in the day wondering whether Vincent was studying her speculatively, before brushing such an idea aside as utterly fanciful and neurotic.

Given a few more months, she hoped that this sensual longing would decrease. After all, she was well into middle-age now, surely a time when many women felt no further desire for sex. She had been lucky in experiencing a relatively early change of life, during which she had suffered from few, if any, of the more usual and physically-distressing symptoms. Yet, as the first year of her marriage to Vincent turned into two, she found her thoughts dwelling more and more on the time she had spent with Alex. Had she perhaps been totally inadequate in failing to understand his complex personality? Was it possible that he *really* had not been unfaithful until just at the end? Why couldn't she have accepted the situation she had so often found herself in if it had meant, as it obviously did, so much to her? Why did she always have to go and act so precipitately? What was he doing now? Who was he making love to? Did he ever think about her? Miss her? Want her—as she wanted him? She had occasionally read snippets of publicity about his painting in the papers from England. But it was about his private life that she felt avid for news. On nearing her and Vincent's second wedding anniversary she suggested that they might fly to England for a holiday and he had looked at her askance. "But it's one of the best times here, Darling. I thought you wanted to do that spring flower thing. What on earth makes you want to go now?" And she had shrugged and lied, "Oh, nothing really. I just thought it would be nice to go sometime." But she had known all along that why she really wanted to go was that she might have been able to sneak off to the Portrait Painters' Exhibition or the Royal Academy, and see what Alex had on show.

For a few days after that particular conversation Vincent had seemed unusually silent and she became uneasy. She never mentioned going to England again and threw herself more than ever into her work. A man whom Vincent knew who ran an art gallery in Paris came down to stay with them, and she was flattered and encouraged by his complimentary remarks about almost everything she had painted to date. It was mutually agreed that he would arrange for her first private show the following summer. Vincent himself was like some proud professor or impresario. His faith in her was being gloriously justified. Even when Jamie

arrived to spend a short time with them while on holiday
from Australia, although Vincent did not, like Alex, resent
the fact that she had a son, he was apt to take him off on
long expeditions "while your mother paints".

"He's an amazing chap," remarked Jamie, one evening
when she and he were having a rare conversation in private
without the company of Vincent, who was taking a bath.
"He thinks the world of you and your work. Makes me
think I'm in the presence of a female Van Gogh or
something."

And she had laughed lightly, before replying, "God no.
Nothing like that. But it's wonderful to be appreciated. To
have that kind of backer."

"I can see that. Incidentally, do you ever hear from Alex?
Or Daddy, for that matter?"

She had paused a little and shaken her head. "No, Jamie.
Neither."

"Just as well, I suppose. I don't take much to the second
Mrs Brent. Glad I've decided to settle in Australia."

When the time came for him to leave, she had said
goodbye with regret, yet resignation. She seemed to be
divorced from so many things now. Jamie was but one of
them.

38

It was different, she kept telling herself, going back to see Alex because he was ill. Illness changed everything. Besides, she was keeping a promise, and it was mean-minded of Vincent not to see it that way. The telegram had made it quite plain: "So ill Dishy. So needing you". It was perhaps unfortunate that Vincent had happened to see the wording, the use of that particularly personal way of addressing her, but it wasn't as if he hadn't known all along what sort of relationship she and Alex had shared. It might have been far from ideal, but whatever else it was or wasn't, it had certainly been a very positive one.

She had sometimes wondered what she would do, now that she was married to Vincent, if she did not have her painting. Could she just fill up the days by lying in the sun and walking up and down the mountains and generally socialising? Merely existing, in fact? After what had happened to her during the last six years or so, it seemed to Sophie that to live without an intense love affair or a *raison d'être* would be like "doing time". Yet there were plenty of people around them who seemed expert at doing it, who really did appear to find pleasure in a so-called pleasurable existence. Mildred Jackson, for instance, with her spreading waistline and unfortunate bikinis, her blue rinses and constant little drink parties.

Of course, Vincent wasn't like those people. He had done something with his life and she respected him for it. It was now only right that he should take it easy and enjoy his retirement. Yet, supposing she hadn't married him? Supposing he had not got her companionship or his very real interest in promoting her painting? Would he have been content down here? Fitted in? She supposed he would have taken up art himself in an amateurish way, as he had once intimated. Or married someone else? There were times when a casual remark of his had made her feel that, but for her, that might have taken place. She knew so little about him really, except that he was genuine and kind and still obviously very much in love with her. She wasn't going to let him down. There was no question of her being unfaithful. Once she had kept her promise to Alex she would return to France. Vincent had sounded so definite about not being there when she did, but now she had had time to think about it she was sure she would be able to get hold of him wherever he was, and make him see how unnecessary his attitude had been. Everything would be all right. She would *make* it all right. She had much more confidence in herself as a woman now. "All we are doing, Hob," she said to the little mascot which she had taken out of her handbag at the start of the journey, "is fulfilling a duty. Going to see someone who is ill. According to how we find him, I might even lend you to him for a while, as long as I can have you back when he's quite well again." She tried to push aside the possibility that Alex might be too ill for the latter eventuality to take place.

She wondered what kind of illness it was from which he was suffering. Who was looking after him? Had he sent for her because there was no one? Hardly. She was under no illusion that there had not been several women—other than Mrs Tuffnell, of course—only too willing to minister to Alex's needs in more ways than one since her departure.

Without his regular attachments, such as herself, and Cara and even Martina, when they had been alive, he would have been sure to have acquired plenty of followers or 'floating doters', as she had occasionally thought of them. Or even a more permanent devotee? She supposed that it was Alex's undisguised need for women which attracted them to him in the first place, and thereafter satisfied the ever-present and overwhelming female need to be needed.

The plane began to lose height over the Channel and she put Hob away while she began to think about the more immediate practicalities. Should she ring the bell when she arrived? Or use the old keys which she had discovered she had brought away after her and Alex's final meeting and which, rightly or wrongly, she had since retained. Today, just as she had been leaving for the airport, she had suddenly remembered them and thrust them into her handbag. They could be useful, supposing there was no one to answer the door. Should she just walk in? Perhaps he was in hospital although, if so, would he not have said? But whatever she found, whatever had been going on and whoever she might discover in the house, she would not let it bother her unduly. Not now. Time had passed, and she was a happily married woman—or relatively so. Whatever ministrations Alex had been currently receiving, she had absolutely no reason to feel jealous about them. Jealousy was a thing of the past. He was a sick man, maybe a dying one, who had asked to see her because once, years ago, they had shared something which had perhaps been unique for both of them. She was simply grateful that he wanted her presence now and glad that she had come.

In the bus from Heathrow to the Air Terminal she stared out of the window as the evening sun trapped the windows of some of the taller buildings in points of fire. Suddenly, she felt at home again. For all the splendour of the scene which she had been sketching less than twelve hours earlier, France seemed so blatant, so relentlessly showy, compared to anything in England, even though this particular part of her own country was not exactly edifying. Yet when they reached the Cromwell Road and more and more trees appeared, when it was evident at every corner that this was an ordinary summer evening in what could only be London, she experienced a curious satisfaction, even elation, that she was back again after some long, enforced holiday.

She took a taxi straight to Alex's house. It was beginning to get quite dark by the time she arrived. The old-fashioned street lamps lit the gardens and she noticed a light on in Alex's bedroom, although there were none in the other windows. Perhaps he really was in trouble . . . yet surely a nurse could have been found . .?

There appeared to be no one on the ground floor when she let herself in and she switched on a light, at once becoming conscious of that curious indefinable air of neglect which always seemed to come over the place during her absences. To her dismay, there was even a vase of old beech leaves, which she had preserved one autumn, still standing in dusty isolation in the corner where she had last put them.

Silently, she climbed the stairs and paused outside Alex's door. Was there really no one else in the house? Was he asleep? Might she not scare him if she just walked in? She had been a fool not to telephone. Then, to her infinite relief, she heard him cough and quietly opened the door.

He was sitting up in bed almost as if he had been expecting her. His face, with its habitual pallor, was thinner, but his eyes, when he saw her, lit up with exactly the same intensity.

"Dishy!"

She went across the room and sat down on the bed and the arms which encircled her seemed hardly those of an invalid.

"You're not," she said, at length, "as ill I thought."

"Oh, but I *have* been, Dishy. Very, very ill. Delirious, in fact. They said I had a virus. Although they still don't know what kind."

"Didn't you go to hospital?"

"Wouldn't let them take me. Saw no point. Made the doctor promise to let me die in my bed. When you get to my age, when there's nothing much to look forward to, one begins to wonder if there's much point in going on."

"Who's been looking after you?"

"They produced a nurse, for a time. And Mrs Tuffnell excelled herself. The higher my temperature, the better she became. Missed her vocation, obviously. And one or two others came in on relief work from time to time." He vouchsafed this information somewhat as an afterthought, grinning delightedly.

"Why didn't you send for me earlier, if you thought you were going to die?"

"Too ill. It wasn't until a few days ago that I knew I was going to pull round."

She drew away and looked at him, puzzled. "But by then there was no need to send the telegram, was there? I mean, why did you want me to come now?"

He pulled her back. There was no mistaking that he had made a remarkable recovery.

"I wanted," he said, as, almost casually, he moved over to make more room for her beside him, "this."

J